ANTHEM 715

By

GREGORY SHADOE SINCLAIR

For our soldiers.

ISBN: 978-1-7374550-1-1

CONTENTS

1. THE JANITOR

I pulled the ID card from my uniform. With a soft *click*, the clip snapped from the ragged pocket. I held out the badge before the new young guard dressed in freshly issued fatigues. The slow tremble in my hand grew, first into a subdued shake, then a quake that quivered the towers of toilet paper hiding my torso and face. The corners of my vision twisted and warped while I swayed slightly, battling internally to maintain control.

"What's your destination?" the guard grumbled, half awake.

"Maintenance closet back in L2," I responded fighting the tremors in my hands. The guard paused, looking up for the first time. His brow furrowed and he shifted to better view the face behind the arms full of paper towels and toilet paper.

"I might be new here," the guard's young eyes hunted for the face hidden in the mound of tissue, "but it would seem more likely that this stuff would be brought *into* L3 *from* L2." The guard cocked an eyebrow. "Not the other way around…and at zero-two twenty in the morning?"

"What the hell!?" My gruff voice barked from behind the tower of tissue paper. "Is this how you get your kicks? Hassling the fucking janitor!?" I moved forward hiking up the armful of supplies as if offering them to the guard behind the thick steel bars. "Here! You take this then! *You* scrub the urine and shit from the toilets, floors, and walls! *You* push this endless sand around the fucking floor with that friggin' broken mop! It's a HANDLE. A piece of god damned wood. It can't cost more than a fucking dollar, but would they replace it? NO!" I roared with hot fury. "How about I sit in that little booth, watching the steel bars rust with my dick in my hand, pretending to be the Queen's guard and hassling the only people trying to get some real work done!?" I spat through the bars at the security booth. "Now, open the fucking door so I can shove this stuff up your ass!"

"Whoa, whoa, whoa, old man…" The guard rose, stepping from the reinforced booth.

"Fuck you and your whoas!" I growled back. "Every six months they rotate a fresh batch of you assholes in here! Twice a year I go through this shit! Don't tell me how to do my job and I won't report you for sleeping on yours!" I laid the accent on thick to mask my foreign voice. My aggression was working. The guard shifted uncomfortably, his common sense and curiosity stalling. I pressed on.

"They just brought you in here without briefing you on 715!?"

"Well, no," the guard replied, "they told us all about the Captain but wh…"

"I just came from there. That son of a bitch built a fecal bomb to blow open the lock on his cell! Do you know what a fecal bomb is!?"

"A…what…? Fecal?"

"It is a bomb crafted from parts from his toilet and his own shit! Did you know shit was explosive!? I didn't! But guess who had to clean that up!? Was it your Queen's Royal Guard?" I mocked in a sing song voice. "Was it YOU!?"

"Sir…"

"NooOOooooo… You sons of bitches just sit over here pretending to be Rambo's miscarriage and hassling the helpful fucking people! Why? Maybe your father didn't

3

love you. Maybe you're just dicks. Maybe because most people just take it. Well not me, Jackass."

"Sir…"

"Open this door so I can kick you so hard they will have to remove your testicles from your stomach!" I allowed a roll of toilet paper to fall from the stack. As it hit the floor, I subtly kicked it in the direction of the guard. "They are moving this shit because they are installing a new steel shitter in his cell and are using the closet for plumbing access! Fuck you! If it was not for me, *you* would be wrist-deep in smoldering shit!"

"Look… Sir…"

Here it comes. I need to be ready. I shifted toward the heavy barred door. I turned my knee out and to the left, positioning it in the way. The guard moved, reaching back into the booth, pressing the button on the control board. A loud buzz followed by *KA-CHUNK* released the heavy steel gate.

The gate, having been bent during a previous attempted escape swung quickly outward. It bulldozed my pre-positioned knee sending me sprawling across the floor.

"Oh sh—Sir! Are you alright?" The guard lunged to catch my fall as rolls of tissue paper spun, bounced, and unraveled in all directions. Like lightning I shot upright catching the guard with a vicious elbow to the jaw. The guard staggered back. I lunged forward with a barrage of strikes that forcefully expelled air, fluids, and wet muffled crunching sounds from the guard who was already unconscious by the time he hit the floor.

Several floors below and on the other side of the building, the lights on the sides of the blue double doors lit up. There were two sets on each side and one centered on top. They alternated red and yellow because someone felt a single color did not convey the importance of this egress. This was the sole entrance and exit to the outside world from the four secured areas of this building. From the corner I peeked around, there was two more locked gates before reaching that egress point. I need to pass through a total of four locked doors. Getting past that security guard upstairs moved me from the L4 zone to the L3 zone.

My freedom was basically a count down from L4 to L1. Each heavily secured section separated by rigid security and thick steel bars. Smack dab in the middle, stood the Security Center. Beyond another set of bars, the L1 zone was just a hallway to the outside world with only those secured blue doors in the way.

An alarm wailed, along with the flashing red and yellow LEDs as the locks released and the thick blue door swung open. Outside light and air poured in, warm and inviting. It has been so long since I have felt it.

"Open the L2 gate also. We need to get the gurney through quickly." One of two entering men motioned to the guard in a security hut beside the entrance. They were medics but like everyone here, they were also soldiers and donned camouflage fatigues. The guard hit a switch in the hut and the alarm changed tone. The blue doors behind the medics began a slow closing motion, the red and yellow lights still flashing. The soldier in the hut mumbled into his radio and shook his head.

"No, open same time," the guard responded in broken English. "You know how works," he told the medics in what was clearly his second language. "They have you clear by the time you walk to L2 gate. Special clearance, just for you. Must wait L1 to secure close before L2 open." He handed the medics a clipboard.

"We got the call from relay. Miko was injured almost six minutes ago. Time is critical." The medic pleaded, signing and pushing the clipboard back.

"No." The guard grinned, writing each medic's ID number. "You late!" He jabbed an accusing finger at the medics who frowned. "And who Miko?" The guard questioned.

"The grub scrub!" The second medic spoke.

"The janitor—Miko… The old guy…" The first medic said as if everyone here knew him. The guard shrugged.

The blue doors scraped closed followed by a repetitive *BANG, BANG, BANG* as the locks secured into place and silenced the alarm and flashing lights. The guard threw the clipboard into the small glass security booth and pointed the medics to the thick bars of L2.

"Jabba's Skiff ready for you." The guard pointed.

The medics frowned, yanking the gurney toward the thick steel bars ahead. Just on the other side of the L2 bars stood the security center. A slanted-walled, louvered-windowed structure. It was dark, long, and topped with one-way glass and cameras that gave the whole thing a striking similarity to the skiff used by Jabba the Hutt in the childhood movie, *Return of the Jedi*. This "skiff" as it had come to be known, was the security control center for the entire complex. It was strategically placed at the converging points of the three main levels of security— right in the middle of the L2. If you were passing into or out of any higher secured area, you had to pass the skiff.

Inside the thick bars of L2, the guard scribbled down the medic's credentials then motioned to the skiff's dark louvered windows. A loud buzz followed by *KA-CHUNK* released the heavy steel gate marked L2. The guard swung the heavy barred door wide for them.

From this corner I was about 30 feet from the L3 gate. I backed up and began to lightly drum my boots on the tile, gradually getting louder until I was running in place, then I broke out into a full run around the corner towards that gate.

"Open the fucking door!" I strained my voice and panted as I sprinted into sight of the gate. "He is going to die! Hurry the hell up! Open the gate!" The guard froze in horror. My hands, one lens of my glasses and the chest of my newly issued fatigues were soaked in wet crimson stains of blood.

"Holy shit..." The medics rushed forward, for a moment forgetting the gurney.

"I set the tourniquet but..." I gasped as if out of breath, running up to the gate.

"Tourniquet!? How the...?" the medics replied staring at each other and then down at their kit resting on the gurney.

"Did you bring one?" the first medic asked.

"No... We brought the impact kit. I thought he fell down and broke a hip and maybe bumped his head! We don't have time for that kit to clear security!" the other responded.

"Shit! By the time we get..."

"I'll get it! Just get up there before he dies! He is losing a lot of blood!" I ordered. Pulling on the huge round bars of the gate, I turned to the L3 guard and barked "Open the fucking door!" Before the L3 guard could respond I shifted my attention back to the medics. "It's in the STK trauma kit, right!?"

"How do you know what is in the STK? Who are you?" The lead medic asked. On the other side of the skiff the L2 exit gate locked into position. Immediately a loud buzz followed by *KA-CHUNK* released the heavy L3 entry gate before me.

"I'm the new guard up on the L4 entrance gate—P9, just transferred in. I trained in Jalalabad." I hoped my pronunciation did not give me away. "Everyone there played medic at some point." The guard behind the L3 gate moved into position and pulled the massive barred door open.

"You two go! He needs you! I will grab the kit!" I slipped through the heavy open gate of L3. I ran forward as fast as I could past the front of the skiff when I saw it. That old chipped dingy tile. I looked away running harder. Dizzy, tired and shifting vision did not overcome the superstition that made me stride wide, over the missing nicked edge of the damned tile.

This was the third time I had made it this far. The third time I was about to cross over this tile. The third time I stood but one set of bars from the blue doors. But this time, the plan was brilliant. I would make it. I could almost feel the sun on my skin, her lips upon mine, run her dark beautiful hair through my fingers, almost touch my son's tiny hands.

"Soldier!" I heard a voice thunder from the skiff. I kept running toward the L2 exit gate. Just this one last gate then the blue doors.

"SOLDIER!" The voice boomed.

"Open the fucking gate!" The quiver in my crimson-stained hands grew to a tremble. I had never made it this far.

"FRONT AND CENTER!" The officer barked from the security office. The words stopped me. My heart pounded. My elation soured. Must think of something.... I glanced around. Two soldiers at each gate, at least three more in the station. Even on my best day this was out of my league.

Damnit.

I moved front and center, a spot in the dead middle between the two gates and right in front of the main guard station. I glanced down at the floor where my feet rested on that damn nicked tile. My heart pounded.

A massive dark-skinned man with a square jaw exited the shadows of the main guard station. Looming before me, I was pleased to realize I did not recognize this man. This was good. This gave me hope.

"Where are your credentials?" the square jawed man demanded. "Who are you?" He sneered not waiting for an answer. Without looking away he beckoned to someone concealed in the shadows of the skiff behind him. An arm passed a folder out of the booth. I patted around my uniform as if seeking my ID card. I found it mounted to my belt backwards. It was placed backwards on purpose. The new soldier whose ID and uniform I was wearing had much darker skin than my own. The grainy low-res photo on the credentials seemed to darken it even further, making even a passing glance a dead giveaway.

"I am Alim" I said, my hands quaking as I slid the credentials into my pocket while feigning looking for it. "It seems I have dropped my ID while helping the janitor. I must hurry, he will…"

"Who is securing the L4 post?"

"No one, Sir. But this is an emergency—and the middle of the night. The gate is closed and locked. If you were not holding me up here, I could get back up…" The colors began dancing before my eyes, and for a moment I forgot where I was. My head dipped and I shook it slightly as if trying to free the cobwebs.

"Remove your hat and glasses." The square jawed guard demanded as his eyes fell to the contents of the folder.

I glanced around. My heart felt like it fell into my stomach. It was over. I would be making it no further. My peripheral vision warped and twisted the surroundings into waves of colors and distorted shapes. I raised my hands to remove my hat and bloody glasses. I bet it was the hat that gave me away. Soldiers don't usually wear their hats indoors. Or the sunglasses. But I had no choice, only hope. Hope that the emergency would mask this questionable disguise.

Damnit.

Stupid….

Frig it.

I pulled off the hat and glasses. The square jaw guard's shocked eyes locked firmly on my bare face. I winked at him, stepped forward and kicked like I was trying to make a seventy-yard field goal. The impact on the guard's groin lifted the huge man several inches from the ground before dropping him to a heap onto the floor. Taking great care to tread on him, I darted into the main security booth as chaos broke out. Shouting, buzzers, radio chatter, fast boots on tile, and the chambering of ammunition mixed into a symphony of confusion.

I jumped into the dimly lit skiff and fired a straight kick to the center of the first guard I met. This sent him crashing backward into another body, leaving both tangled and splayed in the narrow aisle floor. My desperate, bruised and bloody hand skimmed the control panel, slapping the green keyed button labeled L2 EXIT.

"Lucky..." I mumbled hopefully.

"It's him!" a voice bellowed from low and beside me. "It's the Captain! CODE 6! Main guard station! send re—" A quick punch to the throat cut off the transmission instantly. The soldier grasped at his neck as his radio and vomit hit the floor. I glanced through the louvered glass. The gate was not opening. I slapped the green button harder, noticing it flashing a tint of red. Glancing to the L2 exit gate, my heart sunk.

It was still sealed.

"What the hell!?" I looked around when I noticed the L3 gate I just ran through, was still open.

Rough hands jarred me from the back shoving me out and down the short steps of the skiff and onto the floor. I rolled, hearing a firearm discharge. Rugged hands punched and clasped at all parts of me, beating every inch. A powerful hand drove my face into the floor. The edge from a single broken, warn floor tile bit into my brow drawing blood. Thrusting my arms, I pushed up from the floor. A sharp blow to my back knocked me back down. That hurt. It was no fist; someone had a baton.

"Let me go!" My muffled shout escaped the violent pile. "The war is over! Let me go home!" An alarm wailed and boots smashed into my ribs, head, and arms. "Let me go…" Tingly white edges began to appear in my vision. The flashing pain eclipsed even the constant agony in my skull. My last thought before the blackness overtook me was of her eyes and his adorable, dual dimples that appeared only when he smiled big.

2. NO PLACE LIKE HOME

"Try it now!" I called to her. Across the ocean of asphalt, a 737 climbed into the heat-warped sky, the roar of jet wash reaching my ears a few seconds later. With the truck's hood up, I could not see her through the gritty orange rust, but I knew just by the way the starter cranked that she was pissed.

How do you make something like *that* sound angry? I knew she would be sitting behind the wheel, lips tight, eyes narrow, head tilted just to the left with her chin high. I knew because she was at what I called DEFKON 3. It was a pun on the military defense rating system DEFCON, just adjusted hilariously for her name. Anyway, DEFKON 3 was her *angry but in control* stage. She had several variations of DEFKON ranging from the DEFKON 5, *I don't know you*—where she would look at everything around her except the target of her frustration, to DEFKON 1, also known as *Satan's anus*. That is the point where words fail to form coherently and the anger seeps from every orifice in her head. Her actions become unpredictable and rage is just a hollow word that she will find new ways to redefine. Picture this: you have a long, pointy, itching-powder coated stick and decided to poke Satan himself right in the ole puckered asterisk. Think he would be mad? Yup. Now just picture Satan with long, dark, wavy hair. Thankfully, I have only experienced DEFKON 1, once. That was fourteen months ago. I still have not fully recovered.

The engine cranked twice, then the thin wire casing melted off into a blue bubbling ooze that dripped onto and seared my thumb. The engine sound changed instantly from the churn of an ignition to the quick rapid-fire clicking sound of a starter turning without the cooperation of power.

"OK, Stop!" I shouted with my burned thumb in my mouth. "Who fixed this?" There was a pause as she took the time to filter the anger from her response.

"Dennis." She called back curtly.

"What the hell kind of name is Dennis?" I wiped my thumb on my fatigues, then the sweat from my forehead. It sure was warm out, but nothing like the desert I just left, 19 hours ago and a half a world away. "People don't really have names like that anymore, do they?" I goaded her. The old truck dipped slightly to one side and I actually envisioned her arms crossing tightly. I'm OK. Still DEFKON 3.

"He was helping. I was thankful he was there." Her response was clipped.

"Wait! The bad guy from the SpongeBob movie, his name was Dennis, wasn't it?" I yanked the thin wire completely off. It was so thin I didn't even need a tool. It was also still hot and the remnants of the melting casing stuck to my fingers. Across the parking lot and over the water, another 737 roared into the summer sky. "Can you grab the jumper cables from behind the seat?" I said it as if I was asking a huge favor. There was no movement from within the truck. "And my knife from the glove box?" Her hesitation could mean only one thing. I was getting dangerously close to DEFKON 2. From the car seat inside the cab, the cry of an infant emerged. Her anger was palpable, and my little buddy was in the line of fire.

Time to flank.

I wiped my hands on my fatigues and moved out from behind the hood. There she sat, behind the steering wheel, looking angry and unintentionally beautiful. Her anger seeped into everything around her. I approached cautiously.

15

"Look, I know you hate this truck. I know you think you deserve something so much better… AND YOU DO!" I quickly recovered. "But the money we save on this hunk of crap is just more money we can spend in better ways on you and on him." I rubbed her leg and smiled. "I know you want a new car. But we don't drive much, and I think you would be happier sporting that nice tennis bracelet you can show off to all your friends. Just a few more months of saving. We're almost there." An eyebrow hitched up ever so slightly. She was starting to crack.

"I love your guts," I told her. She suddenly looked confused and offended.

"What!?" she slapped my hand from her knee.

"Well, I was thinking about this on the flight. Is there a scale of love? And what is it? I could not think of one, so I started working on my own." She glared at me. I kept talking. "What is the absolute bottom and what is the absolute top on a scale of emotion? Talk is cheap. Anyone can say 'I love you,' but how do you really know what they are really feeling behind it?"

"What the hell are you talking about!?"

"Stay with me for a moment… How do you know words are not just empty, or worse, misidentified? Like lust instead of real love?

"Well, if you think about the bottom of the scale, I can say the most I have ever hated a person was in the first grade—Billy Moyer. He beat me up every day. I hated him with every emotion I had. He was a big reason I started studying martial arts. At the end of the year, I finally reversed that headlock he put me in every day. The next day he came up to me and asked to be friends. I told him with every emotion behind it 'I hate your guts.' I had never meant anything more absolutely in my life. I swear he

16

could feel the loathing in my words." I put my hand back on her leg. Her look of disgust was fading into either intrigue or concern. "I have never spoken a word with such venom or emotion before. Not good emotion, but still, emotion. Everything I felt was behind it. This would be the very bottom end of the emotion scale. Hating Billy's guts. I hate his guts." She still looked confused.

"So, being on the far opposite end of the scale where the mere letters and words fail to capture the true emotion and passion I feel for you, would have to be that same phrase in opposite. An emotion so equally powerful, yet on the farthest end, the farthest point possible on the emotional scale, would have to be—I love your guts."

Her eyes welled up.

"You are so weird," she squeaked.

"Look, K…" She leapt from the seat embracing me with a giggle.

Suddenly a painful impact jarred my groin and jolted my whole body.

"FUCKER!" A deep grumbling voice barked. The voice did not fit in my world. It came from a place that invaded our private moment. My world shifted, then in an instant it was gone. My eyes shot open.

Annnnd there it was.

After the initial agony of impact, there is a delayed wave of worse pain that crashes over you four to six seconds after being hit in the groin. My body tried to buckle as the nausea washed over me right on time. But I could not move. I was bound in place, spread eagle.

Hovering over me was a large dark-skinned man with a square jaw.

"Owed you that one, Captain," he muttered. Then he grinned and punched again.

Harder.

My body jerked against the restraints as the pain and sickness battled for domination. My eyes watered and a baton from somewhere unseen cracked the side of my head. Suddenly everything went white and quiet. My eyes watered and squinted as something impacted my nose. The tinny taste of blood filled the back of my throat with such volume it triggered my gag reflex. Before I completed the vomit, a rageful fist impacted my lower abdomen with tremendous force. I felt something burst.

"ENOUGH!" It was a shout from within the room but I could barely hear it. My ears were ringing and I coughed up bile and blood. Shouting sounded distant and heated. Something jarred the bed several times. I wanted to roll to my side to expel the remaining 'agony soup' from my mouth, but the restraints held me firmly in place. The people in the room were fighting amongst themselves. Probably for the privilege of committing murder.

I was wet.

Bleeding? Nope. Piss.

Wonderful.

That must have been that bursting feeling. The shouting became louder as the ringing, not the normal everyday ringing, but the baton strike to the head ringing, began to fade. I exhaled sharply though my nose and sprayed blood all over.

Everything hurt.

I still can't open my eyes. They water like I am crying. Colors washed over my vision. Then blackness.

3. BRIAN

She was holding him. His huge smile exposed those unique dual dimples. I have heard of dimples, but never like this. People would have one on each cheek, but my little guy had four. Two on each cheek, stacked like tiny snowmen. He was going to be a lady killer with those. She is talking to me. God, I missed her voice. I could talk to her for hours.

"What is her name?" A disembodied voice interrupted. It called from beyond pulling me to a place I did not want to be. "Her name, what is it?" The voice jarred me awake. "You called her K. Was that Kay as in K-A-Y? Or was it C-A-Y?"

"What? I don't…" At once the pain in my head was back. It hurt to open my eyes. Hell, it hurt to move at all.

"Is that a nickname? Think." My eyes rolled and I blinked heavily. Spots and colors twisted and danced in my vision. "What was her name?" the voice demanded.

"K? What…? Who are you? What do you want?" I babbled trying to understand what was happening.

"The child. Boy or girl? Was the child's name Kay?" The voice grew clearer.

"No, her name… No! Wait…"

"The child was a girl? The child was Kay?"

"NO. HIS NAME IS…" I just caught myself in time to stop talking. "Who the fuck are you? What the hell is going on?" I demanded of him. He stared at me, blinked and mumbled a name.

"What? Brian!? Is that what you said? Bullshit. You are about as much of a Brian as I am a Habib. Brian is an American name," I scolded him unwisely.

22

"You spoke of an airport. Where were you coming from?" he asked, his eyes burning into mine.

I tried to reach up and grab him but pain bit into my wrists and the shackles went tight with a loud *CLANK!* I was splayed out flat on a hard surface, wrists and ankles bound. I thrashed against them as a large man stepped forward eager to induce more pain therapy. Another thin faced man behind him reached for a syringe on the rolling table. Brian raised a hand halting them.

I could not tell if my nose hurt, or it was the poorly applied tape that was making it hurt.

"You were travelling alone? Where were you without your family?" He continued to question.

I glared back at Brian. His eyes were young. His hair dark. Almost brown in spots that appeared exposed to long days in the desert sun. His beard too was long and full. I could see why they were using him. His English was good. No hint of an accent. With a shave and a haircut, he could almost pass for American.

"I was just returning from a special *Dora the Explorer* weekend down at Camp Hatred," I responded. Brian just stared at me for a long moment. Then he checked his watch and scribbled something down on his clipboard. "What do you want from me?" I demanded. "Let me go. We are all soldiers. I did my part. You did yours. The battle is over, just let me go. Where is your warrior's honor?" The air in the room suddenly changed, going dead silent.

"Honor?" His eyes peeled up from his clipboard.

"Yes. Every warrior has some type of honor code."

"Explain this to me," Brian said raising his clipboard.

"You don't have a code of honor?" I asked. "What the hell kind of warrior are you?"

"Who said I was a warrior?" He began scribbling notes.

"Your neck. Low, where it meets your collarbone. There are two burn marks. One is a long thin rectangle, the other is a backwards C. Those are burn marks from bullet casings. Usually caused when using a weapon of the wrong handedness. In my experience, this happens most often when picking up a weapon in the heat of battle. Not something that just happens at the range." Brian's head did not move but his eyes left the clipboard and found mine. "From the positions of those burns I would have to say you picked up a left-handed weapon but you shoot right-handed. You have two separate scars," I told him. He stared as I continued. "Meaning you have done this more than once. Soft, sensitive skin in that area. Those scars will be there for decades."

He lifted his pen, glancing at it for just a fraction of a second. Not long, but long enough for everyone in the room to confirm his right-handedness.

"Tell me about your code of honor," he commanded trying to sound as if he was asking.

"Who do you fight for?" I asked in return, glancing at the strange writing on the foreign uniforms. I swear I could almost recognize it.

"Who do *you* fight for?" he fired back.

"Someone who does not use innocents as shields or wartime targets," I replied.

"Who does that?" he asked.

"Come on." I shook my head. "That is probably the only reason you are alive. Who do you fight for? What is your anthem?"

"This is getting us nowhere."

"Nowhere!? Where are we going?" I shouted turning my palms up drawing attention to my bindings. "You mean if I talk to you, you will let me go free!?"

"Small steps."

"Small steps?" I asked mockingly.

"Yes. Let's move in small steps. You give a little, I give a little," he said. I laughed out loud at the absurdness of the comment. Just how gullible does this asshole think I am? What a prick.

"How about I let you sleep without bindings?"

The words stuck center stage in my mind. The glorious thought made me hesitate.

Shit. Stupid, stupid, stupid!

He knew. He knew he now had something to barter with. Something I wanted. One of the mouth-breathing thugs in the room moved forward and whispered in his ear. I could not hear what he said, but his tone was one of clear concern. Brian put up his hand and the goon stopped talking, then reluctantly moved backward into place.

"Answer one question. That is all. Just one," Brian said evenly.

"No."

"Just one."

"I can't." Shit. It escaped while my mind was drawing a scenario of comfort. Being able to place my arms and legs in any position? Curl up comfortably? Roll over onto my side? It has been so long. I think I would drift off instantly. Hell, I could piss myself in glee just thinking about it.

"Where were you? You got off a plane. Where did it come from?"

"I know what you are trying to do. You cannot build a relationship with me. You are my captor. I will never trust you," I hissed. "How about this, you let me sleep without bindings to show you are not a complete dick? Huh?"

"What about respect? I have seen what you can do. It is beyond impressive. You have earned my respect. Could you respect me enough to answer my question?" Brian asked. I turned my head and glared at him.

"Respect!?" I barked. I hated what people called 'respect.' "Respect is not a bargaining chip, idiot. Someone doesn't earn your respect; they earn your admiration. Respect is forged with agony and suffering. It is a solitary journey so painful you would wish no such thing on another person. Thus, you treat others as you want to be treated. *That* is respect. Anything other than that is just a word that ultimately means being a power-craving douchebag." He sat up a little straighter and his brow creased as if actually considering my words.

"Douchebag." I fired at him. The edges of my vision began to dance and shake with colors and twisted images. "Respect? Relationship? You talk to me like we are buddies. I have news for you '*pal*,' you make me want to puke up my liver. I could not possibly like you less, and the only way I could like you more was if you were a urine-

26

soaked corpse." I growled acidly. "Let me out of these shackles and I will show you…"

Brian stood. His clipboard fell to his side. He actually looked offended.

Good.

"Kill me or release me. A captive is only sustained if he has value. A captive's value will typically fall into one of the following categories: bait or information recovery." I recited the textbook analysis from the twisted shifting haze of my mind. "I have no value as bait, and I am not going to give you any information!" I was shouting now. "END THIS!" My voice shook as I bellowed. My hands trembled, twisting into strange positions as they pulsed. A tear crossed my battered face in a slow downward roll. "End me…or I will end you." I gritted my teeth.

"Kill me, god damn it." I was trying to shout but the emotion held it to a pathetic begging hoarse squeak. I had to fight it. I could feel the crushing depression creeping up. Instantly my mind shifted into the easy way out rational. "Kill me…I dare you…" I mumbled.

Brian turned slowly for the door. He motioned subtly to the men behind him. The thin faced man produced a syringe from the rolling cart. Rough hands locked me into position. I felt the burn of the drugs and welcomed the enclosing darkness, teeth bared, eyes clenched, chest heaving in sobs.

"Go ahead…kill me…"

4. ROOM WITH A VIEW

"He's been obsessively watching those teaching videos you made at the dojo," she said, just as the image finally came through.

The phone was a piece of shit and the screen was small, but I could see every detail. The clashing crayoned lines were rigid and erratic. In the middle, backed by a boxy red, white, and blue flag, stood a tan stick figure holding a rifle that if was real, would be the size and weight of a park bench. At the top of the page, in the blue crayon sky, yellow letters spelled out:

UNVINCIBLE

It was then I realized the stick figure was standing on a pile of mangled bodies created in Crayola's finest gore. I laughed.

"Yup. There is no denying it. He is definitely my child," I said proudly. The phone chirped. Another image received. I navigated the small digital buttons with sweaty hands. Three of them were under a loose corner of the glass that had been breached by tiny grains of sand and required me to press them so hard I feared the screen would crack. It was the bottom of the drawing. Blocky crayon letters spelled out:

MY DAD. MY HERO.

I choked up. She knew, filling the air with words of distraction.

"Yeah, well we should talk about that before you get home and find out that the mailman has dual dimples," she said playfully. I grinned and chuckled, swallowing the lump in my throat.

"Nice try. But I know you're not getting any dates driving around in that piece of shit truck." We laughed for a long happy moment. Then she scolded me.

"Don't swear in front of him."

"Sorry. 'Pickup.'"

"Cut the shit! He can hear…. Damn it!" she cursed in front of him. I could not help but laugh. I looked up from the phone. Just outside I could hear a voice. No one should be out here. No one should know wher—

Suddenly thunder rocked the world, and the Humvee was airborne. Fire. Fire was everywhere. A large chunk of the driver's jaw landed on my lap.

Just as the second roll of thunder hit, my body jarred to the right and I was falling. The world shifted and evaporated at once, as if ejected from both the dream and vehicle.

I hit the hard concrete floor. It was dark. The floor was coated with a thin layer of sand and reeked of piss. Echoes of the scream that escorted me from my slumber rang off the walls.

It was the middle of the night. The room was dark, and the only light was provided by the full moon. I was back in this damn cell. Four concrete walls. One thick steel door. One window.

Zero hope.

I exhaled. The old metal shutter in the door scraped open. Dark eyes peered in, then clapped it shut loudly. My head was ringing and my vision was trying to stabilize. I touched my nose. It felt healed. Or as healed as it was going to get.

How long had I been sleeping?

And why am I on the floor? I pushed myself up to a sitting position. Then I came damn near to shitting myself. I raised my hands in front of me. Where leather bindings once held my wrists were only purple and red scabs with a deep undercoat of thick, wide bruises. I turned my hands over looking at them in amazement. Then I turned them over again.

Holy shit. What Voodoo is this?

How did I get out of the bindings? How did I get my hands and feet free? A blanket of bed sores on my back screamed out in relief. I looked at the "bed." I only referred to it as a bed because I could not find a better word for it. Calling it an uncomfortable piece of shit was an insult to uncomfortable pieces of shit everywhere. Whatever the hard, uncomfortable thing should be called, its frame still held the shackles. They were simply unlocked.

What.

The.

Hell?

I reached for a shackle to make sure it was real. Then I noticed it. On the inside of my left arm there was a strange pattern. Long deep trenches rippled the skin. Shakily, I got to my feet and approached the window, rotating my arm in the moonlight for a better view. What was this? It looked like scars. What would cause something like this? It could not be road rash. It was almost like a pattern. Torture? This was the most likely answer. I don't remember this though. I would remember, wouldn't I? Who knows? With the drugs they use to keep me sedated it's a wonder I can function at all.

"Wait!" I actually spoke out loud. "This is a letter! R!" I shifted in the light of the moon avoiding the shadows of the wire screen embedded in the dirty glass. Warped sloppy letters traced the inside of my forearm. What the hell is this? An O? No, too square, looks more like a capital D. If I read it the way I read my little buddy's drawing, it said:

"D-R-I-D-N-K-E-L."

What in *Jack and Jill's birth control pills* could this be about? Was it a message? A code? More likely it was a serial number from the staff of this hell hole. But serial numbers usually had, you know, *numbers* in them.

D...R...I...
Wait!
D-R.
The first two letters were DR. Like an abbreviation. Like Doctor?

Dr. Idnkel? It was a strange name, but this was a strange place in a strange land. Hell, the language sounded like cats in a garbage disposal. So, this mangled alphabet of a name seems like some garbage they would be able to pronounce. Hmmm. I wonder what the significance of this doctor was. Who was he? What information did he have? How am I going to find this guy?

I suppose I will just ask around at the water cooler in the morning. The thought made me smile to myself.

I rubbed the scars again. How did these scars get here? I gazed out the window as I scoured my foggy memory. The damn drugs they injected me with made it so hard to focus.

My eyes dropped down. I realized this was the first time I had looked out this window. I was not that far from a rooftop, then the ground. Just a few floors up. I glanced back at the door. Then at the window.

I leapt over the bed, terribly misjudging the distance. The sound of meat slapping concrete followed my foot catching the bed. I sprawled onto the floor like a drunk tripping out of a bar. Undeterred, I groaned and pulled myself to my feet moving to the door. In a burst of shifting color and shadows within my vision, I ran full force, hurdling the small bed. This time, I cleared it.

I smashed into the window. Glass splintered and shrieked loudly creating a large fractured spiderweb where my shoulder impacted it. Then another a split-second later where my head unintentionally hit. I bounced off the unyielding window and found myself on the floor again.

"Holy shit." I mumbled. This was some strong glass. My shoulder burned with pain and the side of my head was wet with blood. I rose to my feet and looked closer. The wire mesh within the glass was thick and held the thousands of shattered pieces in place. I was not going to be able to break this with my own sheer force.

I glanced around the small cell. A toilet was positioned on the far side. The window, door, and bed completed the inventory. Not much to work with here. I had to be creative. I looked at the door, it was thick steel and swung inward. I looked back at the window. Then, back at the door directly across the tiny room from the window. *Directly* across. My focus shifted back and forth between the window and the door until my sights finally settled on the bed. A large grin formed on my face.

I chuckled. This was going to be good.

"Hold on, honey," I whispered as if she could hear me. "I'm on my way home."

5. WINDOW OF OPPORTUNITY

The bang on the door was louder this time. The door's thick mass rattled in the steel jamb. The distinction of knocking and trying to force the door open was harder to distinguish now. There was a pause. I quietly pressed my right ear to the cold steel door.

"What do you mean you can't get it open?" I heard on the other side. Hey, this was a different voice. Someone new arrived.

"What? You are sure it's unlocked? Well, just open the fucking slide and see what's blocking it!" Oh, this was great. "What? Get the fuck out of the way! Let me see!" The voice commanded. I had stuffed one end of a sheet into the door jamb above, and let it hang down, covering the door. This also covered the hole to the metal slide they used to look through. In short, I blindfolded them.

They didn't seem to like that.

From the right side of the door where I was positioned, I peeked behind the sheet. The rectangular metal slide dragged open.

"What the fuck is that? It looks like a god damned sheet!" He said condescendingly.

"A damned sheet? *Pfffft*," the voice exclaimed in aggravated disbelief. This guy had to be in charge somewhere. Only brazen assholes like this talk down to the real workers with their over simplified and stupid plans that they super charge with confidence until everyone is convinced it is a great and obviously brilliant idea.

I saw the hand reach through the viewing hole to grab the sheet. I instantly latched onto his fingers. Let's show him why his obviously brilliant plan was so stupid.

The technique is called *yubi dori*. While it bent the fingers in the wrong direction making them touch the back of the hand, there was a hidden complexity to it. Some people have hand knuckles like Gumby and just bending the fingers backward does not bother them. However, if you torque on the knuckles in the *middle* of the fingers instead of the big ones of the hands, you eliminate this kind of nullification. No one is flexible there. Now, do that while drawing their elbow forward toward you and they will fall into the finger lock with their own momentum.

Yeah, shit just breaks then.

Yubi dori requires only a subtle "flick" of the wrist to work properly and when executed perfectly, a fourteen-year-old girl can put a 330-pound chauvinistic gym teacher on his knees. Be warned though, you will have to appear at the school inquiry and in front of everyone to take responsibility and agree not to teach your niece any more martial arts.

This *yubi dori* had worked so well that the idiot's forearm shot forward far enough to get his arm stuck in the opening of the steel slider. Before he managed to rip it free, I broke three of his fingers and was working on the thumb. His shrieks of pain confirmed my theory. This was not someone familiar with pain. This has to be someone in charge. He wailed like a little girl.

No offense to my niece.

For ten full minutes this guy cried in pain, until everyone had their fill of his bitching and they lead him off to get some help. He made more noise than the newborn section of a hospital. Anyone not awake yet this morning, was now.

A new group of voices joined the growing crowd outside my door. It was hard to make out what they were

39

saying. Everyone here mumbled. All the damn time. Even when I was not eavesdropping. I just wish they would speak up.

BANG, BANG, BANG!

"Captain?" This was Brian's voice. Good morning, fucker.

"Captain, talk to me. What is going on?" Even keeled. As always. I bet I can break him of that. "Captain…!? No…I just got here." Someone behind him, just out of earshot was asking him questions. The sun was up now. More and more people were showing up. "Yes, right now… Yes, and at least two more of them…" I heard Brian reply.

It was coming together. Soon it would be time. The fingers of my left hand began to quake and drum in spasmodic positions. Yeah, it was weird and strange, but it somehow soothed me. "I don't think that is a good idea." Brian was saying to someone in almost a commanding voice. "You poke that in there and you are just going to give him one more weapon…."

Oh? Please, let's do that.

The voice faded to a mumble again. They must have moved away from the door. Somewhere from the far distant hallway came more girlish screaming. Jesus. It was just a few fingers. What did this guy do all day? Fold paper flowers? In the dojo we would break fingers and toes on a regular basis. Some digit was always taped up. This guy needed to get out more. Maybe play with the boys a little?

The door went quiet for several long minutes. Then, there was a scuffling sound and several voices rose in what sounded like protest. Come on…someone be stupid. There is at least one in every crowd and this place is just full of them. But no one rose to the occasion. Instead, after a few more minutes of arguing, the door went quiet once more.

"Captain?" Brian's voice came through the door once more. "Captain, I know you are in there. Those fingers did not get mangled by themselves," he said. Good point, but mangled might be a stretch. "Captain, I don't know what you are planning but we will not open this door until we can see into the room." Even keeled. Even in the face of an obvious trap. He had to be a good soldier. "Captain?"

"Brian?" I replied.

"My name is not Brian, it...."

"Oh, who the fuck cares what it is today? All you people have weird names anyway," I barked. "Does it bother you that I call you Brian?" Silence. It did. I grinned.

"Good. BRIAN it is. Now can you fetch me a coffee? Black." I chuckled. Sometimes I amuse myself. "Oh, and can you have Bobby Broken-Fingers run out and get me a muffin?"

"Captain, you covered the observation slot with your bed sheet. What do you think this will gain you?"

"It's a game of hide and seek, asshole. So far, you are losing."

"This is not a game. Do you realize we will not open the door? That also means we cannot provide food or water until you clear the door," he replied.

"Bullshit. You already tried to open the door. In fact, I bet the locks are released right now. Aren't they?" I heard rapid shuffling and low voices. I smiled. This was fun.

"Your door is blocked Captain," Brian said. "Please move whatever is…"

"Looks clear from over here! You should come in and look for yourself."

"Captain…we are going to re-secure the door…" Brian began. I laughed. They don't know where the keys are. "And we will not open it again until the view port is clear."

I almost felt bad for him. He had, after all, allowed me to sleep without the bindings. All his fellow soldiers would blame him for this. I almost wished I were talking to someone else. Then I thought of my family and all that went away. This just made me want to feed him his own teeth. I said exactly what I knew would set them off.

"Got it. No food or drink until I clear the door. That is alright. I only need an hour or so before I am done." I tossed the unused second half of the cross-support bar onto the floor. The metallic clanging sound it made as it bounced across the small cell echoed loudly. I grinned, enjoying this. That piece of metal rattling across the floor said more than I ever could.

Silence. The kind that signals the tidal wave of horror that just washed over everyone on the other side of this door.

That's right. I have something I am not supposed to. Something I can use as a weapon against you. Something I can hurt you with. I could almost feel the panic in their silence. I needed them to respond in a certain way. I needed them to want to come in.

The smart choice for them would be to wait me out. Starve me until I cave. I needed to make them want to abandon that plan. Now they know I have something I shouldn't, and I am working on a plan. I have a history of making the smallest objects really painful for them. Their imagination must be in overdrive considering what I could do with something steel and heavy. How did I get it? What was I doing with it? How bad was it going to hurt? Pile on the idea of a plan in progress. That should make them want to break down the door and interrupt my plan before it is complete.

So yeah, I just gave my captors a one-hour deadline.

This made me smile.

About four minutes later I heard the deep heavy thud on the floor just outside my door. The Enforcer. In Special Forces we nicknamed it the "Master Key." Well, because it worked on any door. Once. Then there would be the requirement of a replacement door. The Master Key was a hand-held battering ram. Sixty pounds of mad-man driven brute force that would open or ventilate most doors in seconds. When a Master Key is dropped to the ground, it makes a distinct sound. A few years around one and you kind of learn to recognize it.

Voices. Many voices outside the door. Another heavy thud on the floor. Do they have two Master Keys? Not sure how they plan to swing two at the same time, but heh, bring it on.

The sounds outside the door of 715 was growing raucous.

It was time.

I looked down at my dirty, scarred hands. They shook while my vision twisted for a moment and colors danced before my eyes. I breathed deep. What is the plan!? Oh, yeah. The fingers of my left hand began to drum in strange shapes.

BO-BOOM!

The door blasted inward an inch or two, then back into place. The floor vibrated. Loose concrete pebbles fell from around the jamb. Dust broke free from the ceiling. Yup. They were using two Master Keys in unison. Nice. I glanced over at the window. It splintered, cracking in a hundred directions. I could not resist.

"Just a minute. I'm indecent!" I shouted.

BOOM-OOM!

The door danced inside the jamb. Less unison that time. These guys have to get in sync. The window filled with so many cracks, the outside was no longer viewable. The long metal makeshift pole that was once the frame of my bed creaked under the load of the impact from the battering rams. I spent the entire night disassembling the bed frame without tools. Then, I re-assembled it into a long, thick pole that I wedged one end against my door and the other end against the middle of my window. My fingertips were raw and bloody. One finger sported a tip with no fingernail. It smarts when I squeeze my hand too tight. While disassembling, I came across a three-inch-long decking screw that some fool used as a bolt. They even jammed a nut on the end of the damned thing. Getting it un-jammed was what cost me my fingernail. That bolt-screw is now the very first piece of metal pressing on the window.

BOO-BOOM!

With every boom on the door, they were breaking the window out. Which was breaking me out. I could not break the wire mesh window; I do not have the strength or tools. But I know someone who does. That's right, my guards. You see, I am just managing people. This will have to go on my resume.

B-BOOM!

Every ounce of power they put into battering down my door was transferring through my makeshift pole, to the window on the other side of my tiny, smelly cell. God, I hate this place.

Screw this prisoner of war life. I am ready to go home.

BOOM! BOOM!

"Come in…it's open!" I shouted in a friendly tone with a big smile. The glass of the window arched outward now. I moved into position looking around this hell hole for the last time. Then I spat on the floor. Good riddance.

The room shook once more to a thunderous, perfectly timed

BOOOM!

The wire mesh held, but the frame around the window did not. The entire shattered glass square, still held together by the friggin' wire mesh, launched into the outside world. The makeshift beam fell to the floor of the cell as the battered, twisted door burst open, hanging off warped hinges. One of the men tumbled forward spilling into the room with the momentum of his battering ram.

I leapt up onto the window opening, misjudging the distance, but not bad enough to prevent recovery. I turned and grabbed the end of the torn sheet tied to the pole.

With a grin on my face, I waved.

"Adios, mother fuckers!" Then I jumped.

6. PAIN IN THE GLASS

The wailing of an alarm forced my eyes open. A thick haze fogged my mind. Thicker haze than normal. I slowly began pulling my limbs in to prop myself upright.

What the hell happened?

What is that sound?

Wait.

The window. Once again, I misjudged distance. What the hell is wrong with me? Has to be the sedatives. When I leapt from the window, the half sheet was too short, and the height was much higher than expected.

The jarring stop of the short bed sheet dislocated my left shoulder and sent me tumbling down to the stone covered rooftop below. Yeah, remember that wire mesh window from several floors up? I found it. I landed right on top of the damn thing.

The impact of the fall put my shoulder back in place somehow. Wow. What luck. One in a row! I am on a roll. It would hurt for a few days, but it was functional.

Landing on a bed of shattered glass held together by wire mesh has turned my entire left side from jaw to knee, into a bloody mess. As I rolled off the shattered square, I could feel hundreds of tiny glass shards digging deeper into the muscle. Those should be fun to pick out.

I pushed myself up and my left shoulder screamed in pain. Glancing over, I was greeted by a screwhead. You have got to be fucking kidding me. Three inches of some idiot's bolt-screw was driven full into my shoulder, like someone had drilled it in there. At least it was at enough of an angle where it was just a flesh wound. The arm still worked, but shit, it hurt to move. I pulled at the screw head for a moment. Removing this was going to be agony. I don't have time for it right now. I gritted my teeth and swallowed the pain.

I drew myself up to my feet and instantly regretted it. I almost wanted to lay back down on the shattered glass square. The small stones that covered the roof felt like walking barefoot across a floor of flaming Legos.

Shit. Never thought about shoes. They took my boots the moment I was captured. Assholes. No turning back now. Time to grunt this operation out, shoes or not.

I walked quickly, but gently, gingerly shifting weight from foot to foot. I must have looked like a constipated elephant. I approached the edge of the roof while an alarm filled the sunny air. I had to be on the west side of the structure. It was morning and I was in the building's shadow. I really wanted to feel the sun on my skin. It had been so long.

Looking over the edge of the roof I realized I miscalculated again. Shit. I thought this was a landing next to the parking garage. The ground was actually another floor down, surrounded by more stones and enclosed by a chain-linked fence topped with razor wire.

Damn it.

Well, no turning back now. Pile on the challenges.

Grabbing the edge of the roof, I swung my legs over. My bare feet dangled fifteen feet above the bed of jagged stones below. This was going to leave a mark. Across the roof I heard muffled voices and the jingle of keys. I glanced back to see a door on the far side. Time to go.

I spun around and lowered myself down. Hanging from the wall edge, I wanted my feet as close to the ground as I could get them. Then I let go. The fall was seconds. The pain was devastating. Rocks of all shapes and sizes pierced the bottom of my left foot. I refused to land on both feet, choosing to sacrifice only one. I crumpled to the ground. Dozens of more rocks drew blood, many embedding themselves in my arm and shoulder. However, none reached the depth of those in the sole of my left foot. Blood poured from my foot showing the glass shards how it was really done. I scratched at the rocks in my foot, but several were below the surface of the skin and required digging to remove.

Yeah. This was a good time.

What the hell kind of rocks were these, Cherokee arrowheads?

Voices filled the air above me. Keeping my weight on my left toes, I hobbled out of the rocks and to the fence as quickly as my deep limp allowed. I left a thick crimson wake behind me while bloody rocks tumbled off what could only look like a walking corpse. I pulled my shirt off and slung it over my shoulder. The razor wire was thick. The shirt would not be enough. I pulled my pants off as well and slung those over my other shoulder. Lunging onto the chain links of the fence, I climbed. The finger with the missing nail now added to the symphony of pain with each grip. Funny how it hurt so much less when there was so much new pain, and better pain involved. My left shoulder burned and fought against each movement, the screw shredding more flesh with every flex and movement of muscle. The anguish was complete, inside from the dislocation and outside from the screw. Oh, don't forget about the glass shards. I ate the pain and pressed forward shredding the shoulder.

I'm coming, K.

A firearm discharged.

"Go ahead." I mumbled. Worst case, you wound me. Guess what? Get in line, I am way the hell ahead of you on that front. Best case? Yeah. I have had enough of this. If I am never going to see them again, anyway, let's call this game right now. I am tired of playing.

Reaching the razor wire I slung my shirt over the top of several loops and pulled them down, flattening them against the top of the fence. I tied the shirt to the fence, holding the razor wire loops down. The idea was to take the edge off, not to prevent getting cut. Razor wire is like knife fighting. Everyone gets cut. I pulled my torso up and laid my pants as wide as possible over the squashed loops. Then, placing my chest over the pants, I kicked my legs up as hard as I could, while dropping my torso over. My chest pivoted and rotated upon the covered wire like a gymnast on a pommel horse. Only a single barb pierced through the shirt and pants, but it caught my pectoral and lanced open a long six-inch gash.

Son of a bitch.

This made me twitch and recoil. Losing my form and grips as I instinctively tried to pull away, I spun off the top of the fence and for the third time today, discovered gravity. I landed awkwardly and my vision twisted and faded more than normal. On top of the bleeding and sweating, I could not draw breath. Damn it. I hated getting the wind knocked out of me.

Fighting for breath I staggered to my feet. Pain, loss of blood, or just plain stupidity took me right back to the ground. I crouched and pressed my stomach outward while forcing deep breaths. Of course, they were not deep breaths, they were just gasps of different rhythms. But as stupid as it seemed, it did help.

More gunfire and shouting. The sand just to the right of me exploded. Struggling to breathe, I rose to my feet and began a limping hobble away. This was the best I could manage. I was moving as fast as I could. The sand beneath my feet clumped with the blood to form a crimson brown paste that clung like a shoe to my foot. I lunged forward with raw determination driving each movement. I was free. Outside those damned walls. A grin formed on my face that I could not restrain. For this one moment, I was beyond their control and this much closer to my family. I simply needed to run. The smile faded.

I *couldn't* run.

The fog of my mind was growing, my balance was off, and I was struggling to breathe. Colors flashed before my eyes and occasionally, darkness. I pushed forward. There were other buildings not far. I needed to reach one of them. Just need some cover. Maybe a place to hide.

I began an uneven lopsided pathetic sprint. My old boxers stuck to me. My left side covered in crimson, the right side with sweat. I gasped for air and lunged awkwardly with every other step across the sand. Not far, I could see a street. On the other side was one of several old buildings. My hands graduated from shakes to trembles. I began to grunt with each lunging step. My right hand crossed over to the other shoulder and began digging at the screw. Tears streamed my face when suddenly I noticed it. My hobbled sprint slowed for a tick.

The sensation on my skin was blissful.

The warm caress of sunlight touched me. My head, shoulders and back tingled with a golden touch. Despite the wounds, blood and sweat, it warmed unconditionally, not caring I was a soldier on the wrong side of some line on a map. It greeted me like an old friend. It touched my skin with the warmth of a lover.

Tires squealed from behind me and I lunge-ran as quickly as I could while maintaining consciousness. A woman's voice off to the right, stained the warm air with a horrified scream. Darkness kept stealing time from my vision while shiny flashing lights and blotchy colors streaked by. My breathing was getting better, but my head was light and I could stomach no more pain on my left foot at the moment.

I stopped.

A full-sized SUV screeched around the corner jumping the curb. Its tires splashed sand in all directions as three men leapt from the vehicle. Two men approached with what had to be stun guns in their hands, the third hung back, handgun drawn with a bead on me.

"Holy shit!" One of the stun gun soldiers exclaimed. His eyes were wide with terror looking me up and down.

"Do these boxers…make my ass look big?" I asked between gasps. No one laughed. I have found men bearing guns often lack a sense of humor.

"Captain, get down!" The other stun gun soldier commanded. They moved in unison, the two stun guns forward with the third armed soldier behind and between them, his firearm fixed on me. Good formation, nice movements. I would have to go through the two stun gunners before getting a chance at the handgun. Even an imbecile could shoot me in that time.

"Captain, get on your knees now!" The soldier shouted. I looked at them. One of them looked familiar but I could not place him. They ceased movement about ten meters away. In my current shape, there is no way I could close the distance. My ragged gasping breath deteriorated to a wheeze. I coughed. A drop of sweat traveled from my forehead, sliding down my face where it hung off my chin. In the glorious sun, it reflected back the world around it in a gorgeous, inverted sphere. It dangled for a moment, proudly displaying its reflection before tumbling hopelessly, splashing into the sand below, never to exist again.

I panted, looking around. If this was the end, I wanted to take it all in. One last look.

"CAPTAIN!" The soldier barked. There was only three of them. If I could just close the distance. Unexpectedly my left knee buckled and I thudded one knee into the sand. Sweat ran down my face, glistening in the sun. It felt heavenly. What I wouldn't give to be anywhere but here.

"Hands over your head!" Darkness crossed my vision and it took me a moment to recall where I was. Unintentionally, I swayed. My hands were moving slowly up to my head. About halfway, my left arm stopped. It would go no further. The pain from the screw digging in deeper, the dislocation, who knew the cause? But there was no way that arm was going any higher on its own.

"HANDS OVER YOUR HEAD!" the soldier demanded; his square jaw tight.

"It can't" I said weakly with a slight chuckle. "It's screwed."

"I would love to shoot your ass!" The soldier said. "For this alone!" he pulled down his collar to expose a long ugly scar down the side of his neck. "But that is against orders." The tone in his voice indicated dissension. Suddenly blackness took over and the world spun. I collapsed to the soft sand. More tires squealed in the distance.

"Captain! Captain?" The voice questioned. The group moved closer until I felt the nudge of his boot on my ribs. Then the kick. I did not flinch. Only after he hit me with the stun gun did I even groan.

Asshole.

There are a few facts to be known about this situation. First, they want me alive. Not all of them, but those in command. If that was true, I have the advantage. Next, I now knew where two of the men would be without opening my eyes. This ass-hat was on my left kicking me in the ribs. His stun gun partner would follow proper tactics and take up position opposite of him, on my right. The only one whose position I was unaware of was the cover man. The guy with the handgun. He would be back and positioned between the other two which placed him either at my head or feet. If I were him, I know where I would be. At my feet. It is the one direction I cannot advance quickly.

The stun gun went off again. While being fully aware of everything going on, my body jolted and locked into place. My arms and legs twitched in the sand. My left shoulder felt like it was on fire.

In my life, I have been tazed more times than I can count. The first several times, my brain interpreted it as pain, but the more it happened, the more I realized it was more like a horrible full body cramp all at once. It stole control over your body while leaving you helpless and fully aware. It was extremely unpleasant, but I would take a taze over pepper spray every day of the week and twice on Sundays. Sprays lingered, but not the taze.

My eyes were clenched shut and my jaws locked so tight, I thought I might crack a tooth. The stun gun clicked rapidly as it output voltage. I could feel the leads burning the skin in my back. This was definitely a stun gun not a Taser gun. There is an important difference. Taser guns fired wired barbed leads from a distance. Stun guns required the user to touch the target with the gun. Both very effective, but with the stun gun, you had to be close to the person.

The clicking stopped and suddenly my convulsing body went limp.

I heard a satisfied chuckle.

All at once, I twisted onto my side, kicking my feet hard and fast to my right, skimming the sand while my hand seized the air just above the burning spot on my back. The kick somehow managed to catch both of the soldier's legs sending him into the air. He half-flipped landing awkwardly on his head in an explosion of sand. The sound of electric popping filled the air. Quickly shifting focus to the other stun gunner, I rolled with a vice grip on the wrist and smacked the stun gun out of his hand. Instantly the popping stopped. To my surprise he threw a hard right that I failed to see until it was too late.

The left side of my face swelled instantly with the impact and blood sprayed the air. He threw a left that I managed to deflect, then came that right again.

It was brutal.

Fast and hard.

I did see it this time but could barely move in time to do anything about it. Again, and again he punched, all the while talking. His right was blistering fast. He hammered me over and over. My nose exploded and the metallic tasting liquid coated the back of my throat. I turned into him and rolled to my side to disrupt his perfect angle when he noticed the screw in my shoulder. He punched it.

I screamed out unable to take anymore. He smiled and grabbed at the screw, torquing it viciously in a circular direction. The sound it made was disgusting. Laughing now, he punched my face with one hand and twisted the screw with the other. My vision blackened briefly.

No.

I fought to remain conscious.

K…my little buddy…my family…I need them. I need to see them. And if this is the price I had to pay for them, so be it. I had to act quickly. If I lose consciousness this will all be for nothing.

He twisted the screw and pulled slowly, tearing skin and tissue as just the end of the Philip's head emerged from my shoulder. I cried out. He laughed maniacally right up to the point I punched his hand away. My right hand seized the head of the screw and with a scream of agony, I ripped it out of my shoulder. My vision flashed and dimmed. I clutched the three-inch screw like a shiv. It was covered in skin, tissue, and dripped crimson. I stabbed it deep into the soldier's ribs.

He shrieked in pain, pulling up.

"Not so funny is it, asshole?" I ripped the screw back out and punched it so deep into his right bicep, there was nothing to grip. That should slow down his right.

He shifted, stepping a leg over me and cocked his left. I shot up toward him and drove my head into his left shoulder. His vicious punch streaked harmlessly behind my head. I punched the screw to see how he liked it. He bellowed in pain like an old, rabid dog.

"Shoot him!" He shouted.

My arms locked around him, I pushed to my feet and slid my head under his arm, then out behind his left shoulder. He fought to push me away. He was no longer trying to punch me, instead he fought to get me off him.

Perfect.

We struggled and wrestled. Both on our feet now and locked together, I kneed the outside of his left knee. It buckled. Not enough to drop him, but just what I needed. I had the opening, moving my legs and body behind him. A hard knee to the tailbone drew his hands downward to his groin. I shifted my arms one at a time to retain control, while securing the head lock. This was a blood choke. He would be unconscious in six seconds.

His hands clawed at my arms as the veins in his temples protruded and his eyes puffed and drew glassy. I dragged him slowly backwards keeping him fighting for footing while we closed on the other downed stun gunner. I looked over the shoulder of my human shield to see the armed soldier. His hands shook as he struggled to steady the gun. He said nothing, just quivered and produced sweat. I could smell the inexperience on him. Tires squealed off to the right. My human shield was getting heavy as unconsciousness took him. The blood choke did not cut off his airways, in fact he could breathe. But it did cut off the blood supply to the brain which would put any size man to sleep for a half minute or so. The cover soldier did not know this though.

"Drop the gun or he dies." I commanded. "No time to think about it!" I barked as my shield slumped lower, now dead weight. I released my left arm from the choke and grabbed at my human shield's belt as he fell.

"Too late!" I allowed him to topple, the cover man's eyes leaving me and following his fellow soldier's descent to the sand. I looked hard at the armed soldier.

This guy was so green.

The shocked look on his face hardened to anger as his mouth went tight and his eyes came back to me, but now filled with rage.

Only to widen with shock again. His gun failed to follow his eyes and for that second, he left a terrible opening that I took full advantage of.

"Freeze!" I commanded. He halted, staring down the barrel of the gun I had pulled from my human shield's belt. His own weapon still pointing at the pile of his friends, where his eyes just left.

"Your gun never leaves your line of sight, grasshopper." I told him.

"DROP IT!" I fired a shot so close to his head that it must have parted his hair. He jolted. "Only chance. One wrong move at all and I put the next one in your head." He froze. "Just open your damn fingers and drop the fucking gun!" The weapon splashed into the sand. Time was short, I knew what needed to happen. "I am going to say this one time. You have five seconds to understand and execute! LISTEN!"

I was surprised how efficient he was at hand cuffing his two fellow soldiers together and then keeping the clicking, arcing stun gun leads on the cuffs. The metal of the cuffs was effectively keeping both his partners electrically incapacitated at the same time, while I lunge-ran backwards keeping my gun sights fixed on his head.

I dove into the driver's seat of the three guard's SUV. I slammed it in gear and hammered the gas. Sand plumed in high arcs and the truck jumped back over the curb onto the asphalt. The three doors slammed shut under the acceleration. The truck tore down the street with a long squeal of rubber.

A second SUV roared around the corner into view, racing onto the scene I just left. The cover soldier was still bent over holding the clicking stun gun to what appeared to be a pile of bodies. One just arriving on scene could assume this pile contained the prisoner of war they hunted, but one would be wrong.

The cover soldier shot to his feet, dropping the stun gun and halting the rigid jolts of his fellow soldiers. No longer under the duress of my firearm, he was embarrassed and furious. He pointed straight at my SUV shouting and stabbing the air with a furious finger. It pleased me immensely to see him grow smaller and smaller in the rear-view mirror.

I stomped the gas and sped down the street weaving through early morning traffic. Up ahead on the left was an old, deteriorated parking garage. I jerked the wheel left jumping the median when something in the rear-view mirror caught my eye, terrifying me.

My reflection.

Both my feet stomped the brake. The truck screeched to a stop, sideways in the middle of a multi-lane busy road. I could not look away. Grabbing the mirror, I moved it slowly until my face filled the silvery glass.

I stared in terror and disbelief. Covered in blood, sweat, and sand, the fuel of nightmares glared back at me. I wiped my face with dirty hands and cringed further. It actually looked better covered in sand and blood.

A landscape of melted, warped skin covered the entire left half of my face. Stretching from chin to the top of my hairless head, it reached out from behind the nub of flesh that should have been my left ear, to the side of my twisted and bleeding nose. The left half of my mouth did not open properly looking like the edge had been fused sloppily, then re-cut. Like wax left out in the sun too long, the skin appeared to have run, almost forming drips. The left side of my forehead displayed patchy skin of several different colors, from yellows to oranges with streaks of red and purple.

A single tear rolled from my right eye. Nothing from my left, as there was but a dark hole where a once piercing blue pupiled eye would have stared back. There was no other way to say it.

I was a monster.

Then, something else in the rear-view mirror drew my eye. Movement blurred from behind my seat and silver flashed by. Brian emerged quickly and plunged the syringe into my neck, his shaking hands squeezing the plunger as fast as he could.

"I knew you would take the truck." He stated, his voice still even keeled, only his hands showing signs of stress. I did not even fight him. As the darkness closed in around me, I thought only of them.

And I cried.

7. MONSTER

"You want to name him after a star?"

"A constellation," she responded. "A bunch of stars. I love this name!"

"You want to name him after a group of balls? Burning balls? Of gas?" I jested. She paused; the excitement fading from her face.

"Whatever happened to normal names like John or Mike?" I asked from under the rusty hood.

"I like the name." She replied in a tone that was forming roots of anger. There was a long and silent pause as I figured out just what to say.

"OK, sold. Orion it is." I put the wrench down and faced her.

"Really!?" Her voice was bubbling with surprise and excitement.

"Oh yeah. I'm all in." I said with a smile, wiping my hands on a rag that was so filthy it was putting more grease back on my hands than it was removing.

"Wait." She stopped the cute bounce she was doing and narrowed her eyes at me. "That was too easy." Her smile faded and her eyebrows slid down her forehead. "Why? Why did you agree?"

"What? What do you mean? I like…"

"No! What's the deal!?" She demanded.

I had to be careful here. This was the kind of fun situation I used to get her to flash that amazing, surprised smile. That smile that could melt dry ice. It was really something special and just seeing it could put the worst day in reverse. She did not smile like that all the time. It took surprise, joy, and love to get to that prize. But it was a prize so intoxicating, it was worth the risk. I needed to be careful with what I was doing. This could go sour fast.

"I was just thinking with a name like that, he would *need* to learn to defend himself in school. This would guarantee I would get to teach him how to fight and…"

"What!? You think he is going to get beat up because of this name!?" Her head tilted in confusion. Or was it anger? She crossed her arms and cocked her head to the other side. She glared at me.

Yup. Anger.

Her luscious dark hair was pulled back into a ponytail. The very middle of her thick, dark hairline was centered with a tiny, pointed V that dropped down into her forehead. This was incredibly attractive, but to her, it was a source of insecurity.

"Seriously!?" Her tone was shifting. A deep streak of frustration seeped in. This is not what I was going for. I thought she would giggle and find it cute.

Oops. This might have been a mistake.

"Look, I'm kidding. Really, just kidding," I stated flatly. "Don't be upset." I reached for her hand, but it was tightly interwoven in her crossed arms. "Honestly, I just wanted your smile."

"He is going to be here in two months! You are leaving again to fight for a friggin' desert tomorrow! I have to do this all by myself! Is it too much to ask to help me choose a name for our first child!?"

Whoa.

DEFKON 2. Big leap. This went sideways fast.

I have two options.

One: Apologize profusely now, back off and continue to apologize until I leave tomorrow. By the time we reach the plane she will forget all about this. But I will spend all our time together making up for this.

Option two: Be charming. Win her over with a quick, witty remark that will make her see that she loves me and being upset is a stupid way to spend the rest of our time together. This option is a big gamble. To pull it off I need something shocking that will take her focus out of this situation and reset it into one that would remind her of our fun and loving relationship.

"Alright, look. It was just a joke. A name like that is not going to get anyone beat up." I smiled at her and rubbed her shoulders tenderly. I looked into her eyes with tenderness and sincerity. "I am sorry." The creased lines in her forehead started to lose their tension. This was a good start.

"That Dracula style hairline he inherits from you is what is going to get him beat up!" I pointed at the V in her hairline and grinned charmingly.

The jarring impact ripped me from my dream, rocked my body and even tipped the chair. The sound of knuckles on flesh made a different, muffled sound than usual as it echoed off the walls of the room. My teeth crunched together and the sandy grit of a chipped tooth ground between my molars.

Another punch, rocking my jaw at a painful and strange new angle. This one almost put me right back in dreamland. Sound became tunneled and sensation of falling overcame me even though I was seated.

The next punch was low on the ribs in an upward trajectory. Shouting filled the hot room and registered slowly in my ears. Whoever was punching me was trying to break my floaters. "Floaters" are a term fighters use referring to floating ribs. They are the small ones on the bottom that can snap fairly easily when hit at just the right angle. If you have ever endured the pain of a broken rib, you understand why fighters target them. I coughed, flinched, and shifted in the hard, uncomfortable chair to which I was bound.

I opened my eyes. My vision was met with burlap darkness. Cross hatched specks of light sneaked through the thick fabric of the bag over my head. That explained the muffled punching sound. Shouting and scuffling was all around me. I guess my Mom was right. Trouble just finds me, even in my sleep.

Oh god, everything hurt. Did I just come from a rave?

"You know what he has done to me!?" A man's shout rose above the din. I could not make out everything he said but I made out "surgery" and "this fucking screw." I am pretty sure I caught a "I will kill him!" also. I knew this voice, I thought, as other voices shouted him down. More scuffling and I felt the chair shift violently as if someone in this scuffle ran into my chair.

"I know you!" It finally occurred to me. "I knew you looked familiar. Out there just beyond the fence." The room went quiet except for the rapid scuffing of boots being forced backwards.

"Yes, Captain. You know m…"

"You are the squared jawed soldier from Jabba's skiff." I said flatly. "Are you in charge?"

"I am, you fu—"

"You have a hell of a right." I said cutting him off. "I thought it might have been the fastest I had seen, until I realized you were punching a drugged up, malnourished captive."

"You fucking prick!" He shouted. Then came more shouting and scuffling. "Do you know what you did to me!? I will kill…" Doors slammed and the chaos faded behind thick walls. Suddenly it was quiet. The air in the room was stale, like hot breath.

"He is a competitive fighter. He is quite good. He might have a real future in it." A voice filled the air as the suppressed shouting outside grew distant. This was another, different but familiar voice. "He had a championship match coming up in the capital. Your trick with the screw has robbed him of that. That arm might never be the same. He had dreamed of this opportunity for so long."

Got it. I placed the voice. Brian. Then, at that second, it all came back to me. The flash of a needle lunging from a back seat. That god damned fence. The fucking screw. My monstrous reflection. The full events of my most recent escape rushed back in full gory detail. This explained the hood, the chair, the place I was in, and this lingering dread in the pit of my soul. It all hit me like a hammer. For many long moments I relived it all again.

And again.

And again, until I could take no more. I fought to clear my swirling mind. I felt myself sag into the chair.

It all made so much sense now. It was not just stupid clumsiness or the medications. I am clumsy because I have no depth perception. Depth is something that requires two eyes. Everyone talking in a mumble? I have no left ear. Half my hearing was gone and anyone on my left might as well just mime to me. It was all so obvious now.

So, so obvious.

And so sad.

I shifted my hands behind me and the chain of the cuffs clinked together. Every muscle screamed in pain at each movement. My head drooped under the burlap hood.

"I had dreams." I breathed. It was barely a whisper but Brian, an asshole with two good ears, heard it.

"Had?" He questioned. After a moment he said almost excitedly, "Tell me about them, Captain."

I did not have the fire to tell him to get bent. I just sat silent, sunk into the hard, uncomfortable chair. My jaw throbbed with pain and several teeth shifted and clicked loudly as I crunched tooth pebbles between them. The metallic taste of blood hung in my swollen mouth. The entire left side of my head felt thick and bulbous. My left shoulder ached deeply and my torso hurt inside and out. My left foot was turned at a strange uncomfortable angle to avoid putting pressure on the swollen, wide gashes on the sole. I could feel the crunch of tiny glass shards under the skin of my left side as I drew crackling, wet breaths and the gash on my chest continued to produce fresh blood. Frankly, I would say I felt like a walking corpse, except death would probably feel better.

"It does not matter now." My voice, still just above a whisper.

"Why? What changed?"

"Did you really just ask me that?" My raspy speech rose slightly. "Look what you did to me."

"What *I* did to you?" His voice steady and even. "We *saved* you, Captain."

"You turned me into a monster," I said. My voice still low. Ashamed. For several moments he did not speak. Under the bag covering my head I fought to push images of how my family would respond to seeing me now. There would be no running embrace as I so often dreamed. There would be no long passionate kisses, tearful jubilation, or smiles.

I remember a time when we were driving home late at night through the dark, thick wooded roads of the north. As I rounded a turn, blinded from overgrown trees, a tan fur streak crossed in front of the car. THUD! And it was over. The small deer impacted and flopped across the hood leaving a deep dent and tuffs of fur pinched in the twisted seams. When we got out of the car, we were met with the sight of a small deer mangled on impact. I cannot forget how she gasped, covering her mouth, how her wide eyes trembled. Finally, shaking uncontrollably, she cringed and turned away unable to view the horror that once would have completely enchanted her. A creature she would have loved now disgusted her. The memory haunts me. I cannot stand to see her so upset, so troubled. And worse, I possess no way to fix it.

Upon my return to them, is this what I am to be met with? Is this what I should expect? Would I be the subject that would trigger another such terrible reaction? Would I be playing the part of the mangled deer? Would I generate that gasping cringe? I think back to my reflection and can't help but come the conclusion:

70

Yes.

That cringe. A hand over her mouth as her eyes teared, not from joy, but from horror. I can imagine so clearly, his small fingers retracting, reaching for the safety of his mother, away from this beast before him. Is that how it would really happen? What would they do? How would they really react?

My whole life, everything I fought for, suddenly lost all value. Who could love this thing I have become? Who could be passionate with someone so grotesque? This is a face that would terrify a child, not welcome it. A face that generated recoil, not smiles. A face of nightmares.

Without them, why was I even alive? I lived for them. To provide for them, to protect them. I fought for them. Put my life in harm's way for them. What if they no longer wanted me? What if there was no *them*?

Sure, I fought for everyone. I fought for those who could not fight. Everyone. My honor demanded it. Even selfish ass hats who drove recklessly down the highway weaving at high speeds through traffic like their lives, and the lives of all those around them had no value whatsoever. I fought for them too. Because some people cannot fight and there are a lot of fucked up warmongers out there. Some that are wired to think they have to kill everyone they do not know or understand or who has a differing opinion. Some whack-jobs have to kill everyone who does not believe in their god. I fight to defend everyone from those demons.

But really, if I was being honest with myself, this all came down to family. They were my driving factor. In the end, sitting in this fucking chair, it is so crystal fucking clear. It tears my heart out and rips at the very fabric of my soul.

Everything I do, I do for them.

So, what the hell am I without them? What do I do without them? Why do I exist without them? Son of a bitch, for the first time in my life I finally understood why a person would even consider suicide.

Yup. I see it now. Not only can I understand it, it seems like a damn fine solution to this fucking problem of mine. In fact, it seems like the only logical solution. Why the fuck did I not think of this before? Am I that stupid?

I am terrified of their reaction to me. So maybe the only right answer is that they never see me again. This way I would not corrupt the times we have already forged together. If I die here, they live on with only the glowing pristine memories that they own right now. They never have to know what I have become. I live on through them as a hero, and never become the monster that I am today. If everything I have done, I have truly done for them, surly I can spare them with this one last terrible thing. I can spare them the pain. I can take it to the grave with me, and they will be happier never having known.

I am trying to find reasons against suicide, but the more I think, the more I find reasons to support it. For instance, I don't have to wrestle with who to fight for, or worry about inadvertently giving up secrets to these pricks. No more dealing with the captivity, or this god damned sand. No more concrete floors and walls. No more medicated haze and blistering heat. No more iron bars and shackles. No more missing them and wondering what time of day it is where they are, or what month it is. No more wondering what they were doing at that very moment on the other side of the planet.

Another good reason? No more escape attempts. No more plans. No more resourcefulness or clever thinking.

Not ever again. All done. I will shed no more tears for any of it. For the first time since being taken as a prisoner of war, I was not cooking up a scheme to escape. Instead, I was cooking up a scheme to die.

Fuck these assholes.

Fuck this place.

Fuck this life.

8. THE EASY WAY OUT

"Where were you coming from?" Brian asked. I remained silent. "You just got off a flight. Where did it originate?"

We had been in this room for days.

He had to be pacing. Slowly, but moving side to side in the small room. As he crossed to my left, his voice faded. The twisted hole and nub of skin that used to be my left ear did not work and could barely make out his words. It didn't matter, I had heard these questions a thousand times and just by the cadence, I knew what he was asking. "Where did that flight come from?" He paused, waiting for my answer.

The only sound in the room was the air being forced through my battered, swollen sinus. I sat slumped in the chair, my eye staring blankly forward at the inside of the burlap hood pulled over my head. My one working twisted nostril made a low whistling hiss *"Tssssssssssshhh..."* as I breathed.

"Let's try this a different way." He kept talking. I knew what was coming. It was the same questioning sequence over and over since my capture. I never answered no matter how many times he asked. You think he would fuck off already.

"Your wife. What was her name?" He asked. "She met you at the airport?" He paused between each question. "She was picking you up, yes?"

"Tssssssssssshhh..."

"Think!" He commanded somehow maintaining his even keel. "It is *important* for you to remember." He strained the word important. Was that a hint of frustration in his voice? Next, he would needle me about my son.

Seriously, like a thousand times.

"There was a child there too. A little boy, yes? Who was this?" He asked. "What was his name?" Brian's voice filled the small room. "Think! You must remember."

"Tssssssssssshhh…"

"Remember. Tell me."

"I won't." My voice was quiet and cracked. The words staggered from my bruised and beaten mouth. I wish I could say the tone was defiant, but it was not. Speaking was painful. My voice was small, and the words were a disheartened mumble. "Cut your losses…just kill me." I had said the words before, but only in the terms of bravery or spite. For the first time, I had meant them.

For the first time, I wanted him to do it.

He said nothing. Silence hung heavy in the room. It was interrupted only by the periodic low whistling hiss from a broken nose. I did not have the fire to bark at him or derail the questioning into a shouting match. I was tired. Not just physically, but mentally too. I hurt. Again, not just physically. No matter where my mind wandered to find a place of comfort or peace, all I found was more pain, uncertainty, and concern. There was only one way to rest now.

And there was yet another reason.

Brian was not usually silent for this long during questioning. He sensed something had changed. "You don't mean that." He finally said after long consideration of my response. He waited for me to speak.

"Tssssssssssshhh…"

"I have seen many soldiers and warriors. Few compare to you, Captain." He stopped pacing and stood right in front of me. His voice was close now. "I know you. You are no coward. You are no quitter. You will never give up. You are the soldier I will someday be." His leg brushed subtly against my knee. If my nose worked, I could have probably smelled his breath. He was baiting me. Giving himself up to an attack. Even with my hands bound, no one stood close to me. I was *always* kept just out of reach.

He brushed my knee again. From our position, I have three favorite defenses using only my legs. Two would break the knee. The other would leave him without the ability to bear children. And it would also break the knee. Brian was an asshole, but he was no fool. He stood here for one thing. He was checking the temperature of my defiance.

Many of the tiny square lights that snuck between the fabric of my hood changed to darkened shadow. He loomed before me giving me time to consider the best possible attack. For several long moments he stood there. Neither of us moving, neither speaking. Then he drew back and punched me. The white flash of pain rocked my head to the side and back.

Right in the mouth. My head swam. Fresh blood crossed my tongue as it started flowing all over again. Damn it. It had just finally stopped. I swallowed and slowly returned my head upright.

The cloth bag went tight and then pulled from my head. Light poured into my squinting, flickering eye. I was in an interrogation room. Small, concrete, empty with only two chairs. I occupied one. Behind Brian was the one-way window. In a blur, he punched again.

Nothing.

There was no fight left in me. I slowly returned my head upright again, not even looking at him.

"Fight, damn it." He mumbled challengingly. I just stared off into space, done with this life.

"Coward." He growled. "I thought you were stronger." He backed up and dropped into the other steel folding chair, glaring at me the whole time. "There is so much in your head I want access to. So much you don't understand. Why do you think I ask you these questions?" His voice back to that even and measured tone. He was very well spoken for a soldier. Especially in English. "How do you think we even have the information that we have? The airport? Your wife? How did we get that information?"

I spat a mouthful of blood onto the floor. My jaw clicked painfully as I moved it.

"Medicinal prison." I replied flatly. "I know what's going on." My mouth hurt to move. "We are both modern soldiers." I tried to speak without moving anything on my face. Everything was bruised and the slightest movement reminded me of how each injury occurred. "We know what P.O.W.s are and how they are handled. This is not the Vietnam era. This is not those Prisoner of War camps. You can't keep P.O.W.s locked up for years, torturing them for information the way you could back in the 'Nam era." I stretched my jaw which snapped loudly and suddenly there was a release in pressure and slightly less pain. "Those are costly, dangerous, time and resource consuming. With all the intel and spy satellites, they are too risky to hold P.O.W.s out in the middle of the jungle, or in your case…the desert." My lips hurt when they touched as I swallowed painfully. They were stiff and swollen and my words were tripping over them as I spoke in a barely intelligible mumble. "Times have changed. We use modern medicine and hide P.O.W.s in plain sight. I know. We did it too." Damn, everything hurt. "I bet your commanders got this brilliant idea from us." I swallowed again, the tinny taste of blood clearing my mouth for an instant before starting to refresh.

"Hell, a few years ago we kept one high value P.O.W. in a five-by-five storage unit. He was kept so stoned we convinced him I was his brother and Postman was his transvestite lover." I chuckled unintentionally. It was quick. Smiling was quite painful. "We called him Cheech. The conditions were horrible. Just a cut up mattress on the floor covered with a tarp. A bucket of water in the corner. Doc and a couple of our team would show up twice a day. We would hose the shit off the tarp, the Doctor would shoot Cheech up with so many drugs, he truly thought he was home and we were his family. He told us everything. All kinds of shit. Stuff we didn't even suspect. A few of the right questions and he would launch into full detailed stories. So high he thought he was drinking with the family."

"You don't …" Brian began, but I talked right over him.

"You are doing the same fucking thing." I exhaled forcefully through my nose. Blood sprayed, my sinus burned and for an instant I felt almost like I could breathe better, but a moment later it was back to a hissing whistle. "Only now, *I* am Cheech." I shifted in my chair as the uncomfortable realization hit me. "My penance, I guess."

My mouth was full of blood once more and I painfully swallowed again. "In the beginning… Before I realized what was going on…I must have told you about the airport, my wife and child."

"Postman? Who is Postman?" Brian asked.

Shit. Didn't realize I even mentioned him. In fact, I did not even remember him at all until Brian said the name. This damned medication they pumped me with made it so hard to think. Hearing his name out loud tugged at something deep. I missed Postman. He was my best friend on the team. Maybe not the best soldier, but sharp, deadly, and with a great outlook. When things went to shit and hope was dim, he would spout off about some crazy-ass optimistic plan he had that would turn it all around. He was always positive. His plans might not have worked out, but it kept everyone pushing forward and, in the end, always seemed to get us out of shit somehow.

Heh, shit. Yeah, that was how he got the name "Postman." When he was new to the team, he stepped in shit from the latrine and walked all over command's floors leaving shit stamps everywhere he went. Took him hours to clean it all.

"You stamped more shit than a postman!" Commander said, and it stuck. He was always known as Postman after that.

"Who is Dr. Idnkel?" I shifted the subject. Not for defiance, I just needed to get away from thinking about my old friend.

Silence.

No reply at all. For the first time today, I looked at Brian. The look on his face was somewhere between confusion and the look of a caught man trying quickly to come up with a lie. I let him wrestle with it mentally for a moment.

"Dr. Idnkel. You must know. This would be the one responsible for keeping me medicinally incapacitated and talking. He must be providing you with the amounts of drugs to pump me full of…"

"Where did you get that name?" Brian asked, his tone laced with curiosity. I found the name carved into my left forearm, but I was not going to tell him that.

"You see, you guys are trying to do this medicinal prison, but you are fucking it up. Like amateurs, this doctor is doing it wrong. I have never met him. He has never studied the effects of the meds on me. Meds like these need constant adjustment. Immunity, physical state, these kinds of things need to be taken into account and reviewed constantly. That is why I can fight the drugs now but have no memory of my arrival." I spoke just above a mumble trying not to move my mouth too much. "Dr. Idnkel is responsible for me. Responsible for my meds. Responsible for turning me into this monster." The last words trailed off to a whisper. I had a hard time saying them, knowing they were directed at me. I painfully closed my mouth and swallowed the new blood. I was stating this as fact, but the truth was I was guessing to see if Brian would confirm any of it.

For a long time, there was only an awkward silence and the hiss of a broken sinus. Brian motioned at the one-way glass but said nothing turning back to stare at me. The stark realization of how a situation *is*, compared to how it is *perceived*, often has this effect. When presented with the truth, and all the pieces start to make sense and fall into place filling in so many of the little details that just did not add up, it can stun a man into a deep reflective silence. Brian, who clearly sees himself as a patriotic hero, might have just realized he is the bad guy. And not just any bad guy. He is a big, brown, shit-stained asshole level of bad guy.

Several moments later a man entered carrying a box. He dropped it on the floor between Brian and me and left the room without a word. Brian let out the slightest of sighs and leaned forward opening the carboard flaps. In the box were charred and burned fatigues. Not just any fatigues. Mine. The ones I was wearing when they hit the Humvee.

My chest started to heave as my breathing intensified. Slowly he pulled the shirt from the box unfolding as it emerged into the hell of this world. At the same time, a quiet *thunk* came from the box. The sound of something with weight and mass, not clothing, banged against the cardboard side. My old sidearm? Could I be so lucky? I wanted to look but my eye could not leave the shirt Brian held up. One entire side was missing, the edges framed by burned fabric that Brian tried to rotate into a position that resembled a shirt. He failed. I had to look away. My eye fell into the box again. Why? Because I was a real sucker for pain, I guess. But suddenly I saw something that made my heart jump. Not my sidearm. Instead, a small, thin, shiny rectangular shape covered with a shattered texture.

My piece of shit phone.

"How did we turn you into a monster?" Brian asked. Wait. What? He said *we*. Did he just confirm Dr. Idnkel? Brian stood now, holding the shirt up. He almost looked proud. "I see the man we rescued," he said. My face rose slowly with a look of confused disgust. I had heard the phrase "seeing red" but thought it was just a phrase. I knew better now. Maybe it was a blood pressure thing, maybe it was just murderous rage, whatever it was, it was a level of anger I had never reached before.

"RESCUED!?" My voice suddenly exploded, filling the room. "FUCK YOU! Rescued!?" The chair rocked back and forth as I barked viciously at the bearded asshole.

"Captain, regardless of what you believe, we rescued you. You were injured. You were dying. We pulled you from that vehicle—"

"FUCK YOU!" I bellowed. "You blew the fucking vehicle up! How did you even know we were there? There were maybe three people on the planet who knew our location!"

Suddenly, he dropped the shirt back into the box. His eyes were wide.

"You remember?" He asked almost breathlessly. "Tell me. Where were you!?"

"FUCK OFF!"

"Where were you, Captain?"

"Oh, don't start this shit!"

"I need you to remember. Tell me where you were!"

"You KNOW where I was. YOU DID THIS!" My restraints went tight as the chair tipped again. "Look at me! Every fucking day with the questions—'What was her name?' 'Who was your child?' You don't need to know anymore! You don't have to go after them. You don't have to take them away." My head dropped and turned away. I could not look at him. My rage transformed instantly to a deeply painful sorrow.

"You already took them away. You turned me into this monster. Not even they could want me. Not this monster. Who could?" My voice quivered as the screams faded. "My family...so far away...never stepped on this soil...never fired a shot... Yet still...just another casualty of this fucking war."

"How can you be sure what they, or anybody wants?" He asked flatly. I fought for composure, still looking away, refusing to answer.

"I can help you. We can help each other. Answer a few…"

Fuck it.

I shoulder rolled forward out of my chair and flung my arms like a jump rope under my legs and out in front of me. They may be bound, but they were now a weapon I could use. My roll crashed into the cardboard box, Brian, and his chair, sending each one sprawling in a different direction. My left shoulder screamed out in pain; the screw wound instantly reopened.

On my hobbled feet now, I lunged at him while he attempted to rise. A vicious kick found his ribs but the second met the solid bone of his blocking shin. I swung my bound hands powerfully like I was swinging an axe. Brian jerked his head back just in time as I missed by an inch at most. I aimed another kick to his ribs but he was already on his feet. Brian was fast. I was kicking with my weaker and slower left leg because the injuries to my left foot made it incapable of supporting my full weight.

I exploded forward feinting a kick while my hands shot out to his neck. I would choke this bearded fucker until they shot me dead or he died. The odds favored the former as it takes about four damn minutes to choke someone to death and that thought made me grin.

Suddenly something latched onto my thumb before it could reach Brian's throat. I felt the torque on my middle knuckle—it propelled my elbow, followed by the rest of my body, forward. I fell into the perfectly executed *yubi dori*. My thumb dislocated, then broke with a crack that was sharp and echoed through the tiny concrete room. I

85

crashed to the floor, twisting to release the bone shattering torque and free my thumb.

What the fuck!?

On the ground I lunged my shoulder at him and caught the side of his knee. It was bent, rotating, absorbing the bone-breaking pressure. Instead, he just stumbled back. My thumb was wrecked. Grabbing with my right hand was no longer an option. That was a problem as punching with both hands bound in front was a slow and sloppy way to attack.

I shot to my feet and fired off a flutter kick aimed first at his knee and then in a flash at his jawline. Before my foot could make contact, he *deflected* both, adding power to my second kick and sending me sprawling forward off balance. I crashed face down into the cardboard box. The smell of old fatigues mixed with the scent of charred flesh, hair, and cloth filled my senses. The uniform spilled onto the concrete floor as I untangled myself from my burned fatigues. The smell triggered memories I neither wanted nor could handle. I shook my head as if they would just fall out.

I glared at Brian. Who the hell *was* he? His technique. His deflections. He was *skilled*. Not the way bicep screw man was skilled, with a single powerful right pounding my blind side. Brian had real skill that would only grow stronger the longer he trained. Where did he learn this? That deflection was reminiscent of my days in the dojo. I have not felt it anywhere else.

I rose to my feet, chest heaving, thumb broken, shoulder bleeding, and barely able to move. The door banged open and soldiers poured in. A single white coat followed prepping the needle.

I did not even fight them.

Instead, I subtly shifted the small, thin, shiny rectangular shape that was stuffed into my undershorts. I could only hope it would stay in place and go unnoticed as the medication stole my consciousness.

9. A POISON CALLED HOPE

The instant my eyes opened; my brain slammed into high gear.

The plan *had* been simple. Not anymore. That had all been changed by a small electronic piece of shit device I forgot existed. I never intended to leave that tiny interrogation room alive. I should have died there. Never wanted to see this shithole room 715 again. But here I am. Basking in all its gory. It looked like the same miserable cell I left, but with a new upgraded window. Now, outside the replaced mesh reinforced glass, steel bars vertically striped the moonscape. There was no way I would fit between those. Looks like I would not be going out that way again.

But what if there was a fire? That can't be a safe egress. That can't be built to code.

My sarcasm was quick tonight, fueled by excitement. I needed to be careful. The worst thing for me was hope. In the interrogation room, I had none. It makes what needs to be done so much easier. I should have just finished the job in that room, but…

I had to know.

Somewhere up above the gods smiled down upon me for the first time in a long while. I suspect, rather than smiling down, they just simply ran out of shit to throw my way. It is funny that I am thinking of myself as lucky while I lay in a dark room, splayed on a dirty mattress with all four limbs shackled to chains, bolted into the sandy concrete floor. I felt lucky because I could feel the thin rectangle of my old phone in my shorts. Even if it does not turn on, I had to at least take the chance. I had to know.

One message. That is all I need.

Just one text message.

I need to get free and try to use the thing. It might not even work. Afterall, it was in a damn explosion. I already saw how badly the screen was shattered. Who knows what condition it is really in?

I looked at the thick restraints securing my wrists and ankles. As I had been trained, I assessed the situation quickly, took into account my complete scenario, and considered my tools. Something tickled my strange sense of humor. I had one new tool. I got it from Brian. No, not the phone. It was something far more valuable to a man in shackles.

Binding a captive by the wrists is the go-to way to detain or control a subject, unless the captive has large wrists and small thumbs. Some blessed with this strange combination can escape with a little bit of work. In training, I met a man with this combination. He was amazingly able to slip out of hand cuffs. It almost broke his thumb to get that first hand free every time, but he always got free. I don't have his combination; I have thick wrists and average sized thumbs. I had tried many times to escape cuffs the way he instructed, but if put on properly, I just could not get them over the bulge of my thumbs. The thumb bone just stuck out too far. Until now.

Thank you, Brian, for that *yubi dori*.

Time to put my new tool to the test. I wrapped my fingers over my injured thumb and squeezed, pulling the smaller digit into the middle of my hand and up towards my fingers. The sound was gruesome. The pain watered my eyes. The bone rotated and floated with a life of its own as my thumb flattened out into my palm.

Wow. Brian did a hell of a job.

After my eyes stopped watering and the pain subsided to a tolerable level, I began twisting and pulling my right wrist, and then hand, out from the cuff. It hurt like a bitch. But not nearly as much as it would going back in. That's right, I needed to get the shackles back on. If they knew I was getting free, they would fix it. So, I would do what I needed to, and then return to the shackles voluntarily, or until it was time to finish my "job."

After several excruciating minutes, my right hand was free. Covered in sweat and breathing like I just sprinted a mile, I reset the thumb the best I could and struggled with the cuff on my left hand. It was not easy loosening it with a bad thumb. The thing was damn near useless and it felt like it had been run over. Twice.

I had to pause a few times to avoid being ill.

I hated that. There were different types of pain. Muscle pain or structural pain. Muscle, like a pull or wound. Structural, like a broken bone. They had their own feel and if one could learn to recognize them, one could become quite adept at finding their very limits and then carefully pushing past them to grow stronger. Some sick bastards like myself grew to enjoy the muscular pain that came with pushing the limits. However, the structural pain of a broken bone…that was hard to love. It was a very different pain and it always made me nauseous.

My stomach turned again. I owed Brian. Asshole. If I ever get a hold of him, I will beat him to death. Although, you had to admire his skill. He clearly knew his stuff. I gripped the buckle of my left shackle and began working it loose. My thumb gripped and I winced. Know what I could use right now? Adrenaline. Pain was so much easier to deal with when under the effects of adrenaline. For me it was better than any medication.

Two more winces and the buckle finally came loose.

I pulled my left hand free and sat up. Immediately I drew the black device from my dingy shorts. I moved it carefully, slowly, rotating it in the moonlight like it was a grenade in a nitroglycerin plant.

What the hell was I doing?

I flipped it over. A spiderweb of cracks covered every inch of the screen. Two crusty splotches of old, dried bloody fingerprints stained the shattered surface. I noticed the top left corner seemed to be slightly concaved as well. This damned thing had seen better days. I rotated it in my hand again and my finger found the familiar power button. I froze like it had just pulled a gun on me.

Please, god—please. Tell me the battery has some sort of charge. I took a deep breath and pressed the button.

Yep, the gods must have run out of shit. The screen illuminated and bizarre foreign letters danced across the shattered display. The top left corner was a green and red pixelated mess. I can work with that. The foreign alphabet displayed on the screen was strange as it flashed by. Some of the letters looked English, others letters…Were they even letters? Who the fuck knows? Did they try to crack this phone? Did they corrupt it? Probably not. It looked like the same weird alphabet the guards had on the uniforms.

Fuckers.

After several long moments I was greeted with a lock screen. Behind the unusual writing and keypad, illuminated a picture of her face. Smiling and beautiful. Not a care in the world. Her thick dark hair was down. Curly locks danced in the gentle breeze. Her eyes were warm and inviting, lips parted in a delicate smile that exposed the slight snaggle of her right tooth. She wore that replacement red shirt. It had been just after Halloween. I bumped into her and got grease on her yellow one while trying to get that fucking truck running again. I picked her up that red one later that afternoon. I think it might have been the last thing I gave her.

I drank in every pixel of the background image. I could stare at this picture for days without ever taking my eyes away. She was more beautiful than I remembered. The perfect woman.

God, I missed them.

I couldn't do this. I pulled my eyes away. This was not helping me. I know what has to be done and this was not making it easier. I squeezed the phone. This was an incredibly stupid idea. Monumentally stupid. I glanced to the top right of the phone to check the remaining battery.

"Shit." The word left my mouth before I could stop it. The small number on the top next to the battery icon read sixty-four percent. I poked the screen. I was suddenly presented with a sentence written in some fucked up language and below it, a three-by-four grid, most likely numbers. What the hell kind of alphabet was this? Some English letters mixed in with other…symbols?

Wait.

In any language, I knew what this screen was asking for. A passcode.

What was the passcode?

"Oh shit."

I stared at the screen. My mind raced. What was it? I had no recollection of what it could be. None. I thought as hard as I could. Was it a date? Anniversary? Lucky number? Fucking hat size? Jesus, it could be anything.

"Shit." I said again.

I stared at the screen, memorizing each letter and marking on the number pad. Then powered the phone off. The room went dark as the screen winked out. I need to stop. I need to stop right now.

Right.

Fucking.

Now.

I needed to get a grip on my situation and lose this very dangerous, very poisonous thing called hope. I know how this turns out. I know how this ends. There is no loving embrace with a symphony playing us off into the sunset. No happily ever after. All chances of that ended when Dr. Idnkel butchered my face. My world consists of my wife and son who are half a planet away in a tiny, beat up, paint peeling, leaky radiator, mildew-smelling apartment with a piece of shit truck that was ready for the dump six fucking years ago. She is a gorgeous woman waiting for the return of her handsome husband, not the grotesque patchwork man I have become. I am the epitome of the bait and switch scam. I don't resemble the man she married or fell in love with. I barely resemble a man at all. I can't go back there. What kind of position would that put her in? I could not do that to her. No good could come out of it. I would not wish that situation on my worst enemy. I would not even wish that on Brian. I just cannot do that to her. That thought alone stole my breath. No words exist that could accurately describe the depth of that hurt. A pain I could feel into my very soul. I drew a deep breath and laid back.

I think I just had an epitome; my life comes down to only two items of value. Two. That is all.

My wife and my son.

The reality of that realization is sobering. Not that I care or place value on any possessions. I do not. My happiness has, and always will require only those two people. I could live in a cave with them and be truly, honestly happy. But would they be? Another thought that was like a knife deep through the heart. I, the man of the house, could not provide for them. I could not give them a better life. In fact, I wonder if her life was better before I came into it? With horror, it occurred to me, it was. I took her from her parents' home. From the comfort of family and the things a lifetime of well earning parents provided. She had a swimming pool. She had a washing machine that worked without a use of a board and bungie cord.

What does that say about me as a husband? As a man? What kind of life can I provide for my son? Here I sit, with the only thing of value to offer them is my absence. That is all. My best gift. I have nothing more of worth to offer them or the world.

I am a broken, failure of a man. And that realization completely drained that poison called hope from me.

I squeezed the thin black brick in my left-hand, gritting what teeth I had left. What would my text message say? Even if I could remember the passcode? What do you say to someone who only knows you for who you were before you became sub-human? The thought made my stomach turn like I just broke a bone.

This was a very bad idea.

I freed my ankles from their shackles and rose unsteadily to my feet. I needed to find a place to hide this phone. Whatever I was going to do with it, I needed more time to think. Where in the cell, could I hide it? I could put it under the mattress, or better yet, in it. However, that would run the risk of it being found or worse—broken. It was barely working now and would not take much to push it past the broken-beyond-usable point.

Let's consider the mattress Plan Z. But what else was there? I was in a concrete block with a mattress and a toilet. Everything was concrete. The floor, the walls, the…. The…. I looked up and my jaw dropped.

I moved over to the toilet and carefully stood on it. Stretching out as far as possible, I could just reach the light in the middle of the ceiling. The *drywall* ceiling. That is right, DRYWALL.

Someone fucked up.

I stretched out and grabbed a hold of the light fixture. I was angled so far out, the only thing keeping me from belly flopping onto the concrete floor was my grip on the porcelain fitting. It held all my weight.

With all my might, I rocked sharply forward.

It moved.

I grinned.

I rammed it with every ounce of my weight. Back and forth I rocked against it with all my force. Back and forth. Back and forth. With each shift it moved slightly more and more. I did this until I could see the hole cut in the sheetrock for the light housing box. It reached the point where it would shift a few inches, exposing a round hole around the fixture about an inch wide at the apex.

Perfect.

The mattress was hard to tear, but I managed to make a small hole. This was harder than it sounds. Being right-handed with a broken thumb means a lot of working with my awkward left hand. And cursing. A lot of cursing. After enough to offend a sailor, I ripped a spring free.

Using the small flow holes around the top of the toilet bowl, I bent one end of the spring as straight as I could. It was damn resilient, but I got it enough for this purpose. Then, using the rough concrete of the floor, I filed down the point and what little bit of the edge I could. It took hours and the sun was beginning to chase away the black night sky. Soon, guards would come in and inject me. Once I was unconscious, they would search and inspect the cell. Then, they would release my bindings and leave some "food" laced with more drugs. I would be unconscious again not long after I ate. Sometime later I would awaken shackled back to that fucking mattress where I would remain until the next "meal" and inspection. This was the mechanics of my life with only daily visits from Brian and his intel questions to break up the routine.

The thought of enduring another day of this triggered my desire to use the spring knife to slit my wrists.

I wish that were a joke.

But I tried.

While the sharpened end of the spring will be fine with shaving drywall, it did little more than deep scratch my wrists. Sure, it easily broke the skin, but it could not get deep enough to get through the veins. The blood made the spring slippery and cutting with pressure was nearly impossible.

After using toilet water to clean up the bloody mess, I returned to the light fixture. I jammed the spring knife in the space between the fixture housing and the ceiling drywall. Then I began to cut.

What a pain in the ass. It was really more of shaving small pieces away than real cutting. Whittling away one tiny flake at a time. Even when I got a good piece, it was still tough because the spring knife was just not great for leverage, so it was slow going.

All this time carving sheetrock, I held myself up with the four good fingers of my right hand. I felt like I was trying to climb a pole with thumbless mittens. I shaved and carved and shaved and carved. Little white flecks fell to the ground while other smaller particles danced through the air, descending like tiny snowflakes in winter. I needed to hurry. The early morning sun was beginning to cast shadows into the room. My time was short.

I widened the hole almost enough to slide the phone up next to the housing. I hopped off the john and looked up at the round hole.

It was no longer round. It now had two square corners.

Shit.

"Have you ever tried to cut a round hole with a straight blade?" I mumbled angrily to no one.

You know how everyone has at least one strange quirk? Yeah. Round holes? That is mine. Can't do it. They always end up square. Then I try to fix it, and it comes out as a rounded square twice as big as I planned. I don't know, but I just can't cut or carve anything round. It will always come out square. Yes, that is my handicap.

Damn it. That's not going to do. Round would look natural, hard to notice, but this…this looked like someone wedged a round light in a square friggin' hole. Or, more accurately, it looked like someone is trying to make a hidey-hole.

I hopped back up on the toilet, stretched out for the fixture. I began carving to round out the hole. Seriously, what the hell was it with…

The fixture shifted unexpectedly. The thumbless grip of my right hand suddenly slipped and resistance was gone. I streaked headfirst down to the floor as my foot caught the edge of the toilet seat. The concrete rushed up faster than my hands could come down to brace for impact. The crack of a skull on the hard floor rung for a split second before that blinding flash of light that occurs from a jarring impact, faded into darkness, taking me with it.

10. A ROUND HOLE WITH A STRAIGHT BLADE

"This smells like a skunk barfed on it." My face contorted and nose turned up. "After he took a shit inside it." She fought to stifle a smile.

"Well, you should have picked them up before they turned." She smirked with a 'let the punishment fit the crime' look.

"Whoa, I thought the stem smelled bad. Smell its asshole." I flipped the pumpkin over and held it up for her to smell.

"Pumpkins don't have assholes! That is just the bottom." She pushed it away, unable to hold back the smile. "Just carve the thing!"

"Carve it?"

"Yes. Carve a face. The eyes, nose, mouth. Haven't you ever carved a pumpkin?"

"No."

"Really? How can that be?"

"My parents hated kids." I replied only half joking.

"Shut up! That is not true!" she said with a giggle, but stopped from pressing the issue. I did not either. It was an uncomfortable subject for both of us. I lived with it, knowing and keeping their dirty little secrets. She lived trying to pretend things like that did not happen. She wrestled with knowing what those people that she called 'parents-in-law' had done. Stuff that only happened in stories or to other people. We spoke of it only a few times.

I had to tell her before we committed our lives together. It sucked, but I did. Just speaking the words brought on the shakes and cold sweats. Our conversation was brief, and I had to leave afterward. Those kinds of memories put me in a sick state of mind. Over time she would timidly ask a detail like what triggered it or how they hid it from others. I would reply in curt, clipped, matter-of-fact responses. It was like briefing up the chain of command. Then, I would promptly change the subject.

I never felt welcomed in my home as a child. It was clear my parents had children for one reason. They needed workers. The farm was a big place and there were lots of jobs that needed to get done. Children were cheap labor and they are fun to make. But when the work was done, things broke down. Often badly. My father was a mean old son-of-a-bitch that was never happy. A violent man who was miserable and wanted nothing but for others to be just as miserable. As a scrawny, undersized child, he was the real reason I started martial arts training. Of course, I always lied and told others it was for protection from a bully at school, but the truth was I needed it for the one guy in the world for whom you should never need it.

I lived the martial arts. It was my escape. While my hands were busy, my mind drilled techniques, reversals, counters and attacks during those countless long days in the barn or the fields. When jobs were complete or the sun had set, I trained endlessly on the outskirts of the fields, along the tree lines. Shadowboxing, forms, stretching, repetitive striking; I practiced mentally and physically until exhaustion overtook both. I was obsessed with the arts and worked my strategies like a chess master, figuring out a counter to every attack and then how to use each counter against an opponent.

It would be over a decade before I turned that skill against the angriest, most miserable man alive. At the age of sixteen, we went toe to toe "like men" as he called it. After I broke his nose and two teeth, I pulled the keys from his pocket and drove off with his piece of shit truck, never to return to that place. He never came for the truck. I never expected him to. I knew how that old bastard thought.

It was my trophy.

I found myself looking out the window at that same piece of shit truck parked out front. I looked away, ignoring the knot in my stomach.

"Well, it's you and me, smelly pumpkin," I said and then got started carving. Using the chef's knife, I worked at the thick orange shell. I was focusing on trying to keep all the features straight and proportioned while not cutting anything off myself with the huge blade of the knife. The odor was bad, and carving was much more challenging than just stabbing some holes. The retching from the increasingly foul stench made this an experience I would not soon forget.

"There," I said sometime later, "Not bad."

"What the hell is that!?" She was holding her hands up, palms out, almost defensively—as if the pumpkin was threatening her life.

"It is Orion! See, one tooth…smile…slight foul odor…I think I nailed it…" I chuckled.

"His eyes. Is he wearing square glasses?"

"Glasses?" I looked back at the smelly pumpkin. "No. Why?"

"Why are his eyes square?" She pointed while tracing squares around her own eyes.

"Have you ever tried to cut a *round* hole with a *straight* blade?" I replied in my defense.

"I have made Jack-O-Lanterns before and they have never looked like that. It's weird," she said.

"It's Halloween," I shrugged. "Halloween is weird."

"No. Here, let me fix it…" She reached for the knife when her face contorted. She had caught a whiff of the disgusting thing. I looked at her and then at the pumpkin. I sighed and pulled it toward me.

"Wait…I will fix it." I mumbled conceding, but not happy about it. "Fine. Round eyes… Even though that sounds racist…"

I drew the huge knife and began carving away, whittling at the corners. Again, I was using a straight blade. It just is not easy to make a *round* circle with a *straight* blade. I worked the foul-smelling pumpkin for some twenty minutes until I was up against my 'urge to murder' threshold.

"Ta-da!" I proclaimed. She rewarded my efforts with:

"What the hell?"

"What's wrong now? They are round!" I pointed out the two enormous round eye holes that overpowered the entire pumpkin. The round eyes were so big they overlapped in the center of the face and just missed encompassing the mouth. The nose was gone now, overtaken by the huge eyes. "They might be a little oversized, but I had to carve a lot to get them round."

"It looks like an ass." She said flatly. My head snapped back to the pumpkin and I opened my mouth in rebuttal, but the sight made me squint and cock my head. The huge round eyes jammed together suddenly no longer looked like eyes to me.

"It looks like a fat Oompa Loompa is pressing his bare ass up against a window," she said. And she was totally right. There was no denying. I had made an ass of this pumpkin.

"You are just confused. You see, the shit smell..." I tried to quickly develop an angle to change her mind.

"We are not putting that in the front of the house."

"But...I...It's my first Jack-O-Lantern..." I stammered.

"It's not a Jack-O-Lantern," she said.

"It's a Jack-*Ass*-O-lantern."

For a brief moment we stared at each other wordlessly. Then as if on cue, we burst out in laughter. We roared until our eyes streamed tears and we woke Orion from his afternoon nap.

Ka-clunk...ka-clunk...ka-clunk.... The sound invaded the comfort of our laughter pulling me from the joy of her presence and humor. I knew the sound. It was far off but growing ever closer. It made my stomach seize and my digestive tract ache. My eyes shot open.

Shit.

The food cart.

I tried to pull my head off the gritty concrete floor. The deep, thick tapestry of pains I felt wove from unconsciousness all the way to my waking body. There were layers of complex agony ranging from the thick and swollen new injuries, to the stiff old healing ones. Each screamed out with my every move. My head felt like it weighed two tons. It pounded, hurting in ways I could not describe in my confused and hurried state. I touched it and found a huge new lump where it had impacted the floor. My vision twisted and nausea rose as the taste of bile filled my mouth.

Ka-clunk…ka-clunk…ka-clunk….

They were close. When they reached my door, they would slide the metal shutter open to ensure I was secured in shackles. Then they would unlock the door, enter my cell, and drop my food while doing a quick inspection of both me and the room. Finally, they would shoot me up with drugs to put me under. Once unconscious, they would release my shackles and exit.

I scrambled forward in a rapid crawl leaping onto the hard, uncomfortable mattress. I flipped onto my back, landing spread eagle with my hands and feet where the shackles would have held them. The *SHHHHINK!* of the metal shutter sliding open filled me with panic. I had made it back to the bed and was in position, but I was not really shackled down.

Please don't notice… Please don't notice…

If I were a better man, I would say a prayer.

I held my arms and legs in position with the shackles beneath them. I did not turn my head to look. Every second seemed like an eternity. *SHHHHHOCT!* The sound of the slide closing finally came. The jingle of keys. The mumble of voices. I had seconds to get back in the shackles. I moved with the speed of a teenager undressing on prom night. Left ankle…in…buckled…done! Left wrist in…clip in the belt… The keys stopped jingling and the sound of a metal key hitting the lock filled the hot morning stench of the room.

"SHIT!" I hissed as I jammed my broken thumb. My eyes watered as I pushed through the pain and buckled the left wrist shackle into place. The lock tumblers clicked into place and released the heavy metal door. I was out of time. I flung myself flat onto my back, my right wrist and ankle still free. In one quick painful motion I pulled my injured thumb into the center of my palm and jammed my hand deep into the shackle. The pain made my whole body flinch as the broken digit compressed into the still-buckled shackle. I had pulled free of this one earlier and never unbuckled it. It turns out that was smart, as the door opened. I worked my throbbing right hand subtly, pushing it deeper and deeper until my fingers emerged out the other side and the shackle reached my wrist.

Two men with stun guns drawn entered the small stuffy room and encircled me. I wondered if they did this for everyone here, or if I was special.

"What the hell?" The guard at my feet exclaimed, motioning to my free right leg. "Don't move, Sir! Don't move!" He commanded, crouching and grabbing my ankle. He slammed it down on the mattress, flipping the shackle around it. His eyes darted back and forth from me to the shackle as he fought to quickly secure the restraint. The guard on my left kept just out of reach with his stun gun fixed on me.

"How did you get that free?" He stood, pointing to my newly bound right leg.

"What!?" I asked. "What the fuck is wrong with you? Really? How could I have possibly gotten that shackle off with both my hands and my other leg tied down. I can't even sit up to reach it. Seriously, it must have been a real struggle for you to maintain a solid D-average in school." My head swam, pounding with throbs of pain while my stomach turned with nausea.

"Then how did you get that leg free!?" He shouted pointing at the shackle.

SHIT.

SHIT, SHIT, SHIT.

I just noticed it. The phone was on the edge of the toilet. Right where I left it before I swan dived face first into the concrete floor. I needed to keep their eyes on me. I needed to create a scene that would keep their focus on me and forget to even check that side of the room.

"Look genius, it seems like the only logical scenario is that whoever put that shackle on last night did not do it right." I glared at him. "Because if I could get that leg free on my own, I would have broken it off in your ass already."

He sighed and looked at his partner who finally lowered his stun gun and turned to retrieve the "food" from the cart in the hall.

"I need Dr. Idnkel. Go get him. I have to talk to him about my medication." I commanded. The guard was a good-sized black man. He looked mean and sweaty. He stared back at me and shook his head ever so slightly as he rolled his eyes.

The other guard re-entered the room. He dropped the tray on the floor and slid it with his foot up to the mattress. A third man with the syringe entered the room mumbling something. The guards took position on both sides. This was it. After this, the only thing left for them to do was the room inspection. I had to act now.

The needle entered my arm and just as the man was depressing the plunger, I yanked my elbow in sharply. The needle broke off just below the barrel, spilling the medication everywhere. Instantly blood began spurting outward in a pulsing spray from the needle still lodged in the vein in my arm. All three grabbed for it trying to cover and stop the spray of blood from shooting everywhere. I threw my body back and forth pulling, pushing, and wiggling my elbow free of their every attempt. There was shouting now and all three of us were covered in crimson. It must have been on the floor as well, because even though they were all on their knees, they were slipping, sliding around trying to gain leverage and position.

"CODE SIX!" The syringe man started shouting as the large black soldier started punching me. His first shot to the head was jarring and I think I blacked out. My vision swirled and my stomach turned, dry heaving into a cough. Another shot to the head and now I could hear shouting, but it sounded as if it were coming from a long tube. I tried to fight, I tried to pull my elbow back in… Wait…what was that? Another needle? Damn it.

I twisted and threw my body side to side. Faintly, I could hear them shouting but I could see nothing. Where my eyes even opened?

Why was I cold?

11. SPECIAL DELIVERY

"GET DOWN! GET THE FUCK DOWN!"

I sat bolt upright. My hands shot out in front of me in a defensive position.

"LEFT FLANK! FORWARD NINE O'CLOCK!" panicked shouting bit into my groggy state. It was dark and I was cramped in some kind of crate. To my right in the blackness was a small, barred window about two feet square. Even with the loss of my left ear, I could tell the voice was coming from the other side of those steel bars.

"CAPTAIN! MAN DOWN! MAN DOWN! WE NEED TO GET OUT OF HERE!" A body slammed the bars of the window as it thrashed side to side. I looked around trying to gain my bearings as the colors swirled in my vision and the objects before me warped with each movement. I felt foggy and sick. I leaned into the barred window.

"Calm down…take it easy…we are OK." I tried to comfort the writhing man.

"FALL BACK! FALL…" His shout was startling. My left hand shot through the bars and grabbed at the soldier. I pulled his sleeve so hard it ripped off at the shoulder.

"SOLDIER!" I commanded in a powerful voice. "GET A HOLD OF YOURSELF!"

Suddenly the thrashing and shouting stopped.

"YES, SIR!" He replied sharply sitting up as if at attention. I released the torn sleeve and it fell to gather at the man's wrist. On his arm, a large, wide Z-shaped scar traced around his bicep. The strange placement reminded me of a uniquely shaped tattoo I had seen before. Many times before. The wavy lines followed by a circle that mocked the stamp of a postal mark. I squinted at the man's face. It was dirty, the hair was longer, matted and for the first time I saw him with a thick beard. But the eyes…I swear I knew them… Were they? Could it be? They were not exact, but it was dark and we had been through so much. Those eyes now looked troubled and heavy with pain and deep regret. I was almost sure I knew them…

"Postman?" My voice caught his attention and his eyes fixed on mine. Through the darkness I could almost feel his gaze. I gripped the bars and pulled my face right up to them for a better look at the man. He squinted.

"Who in the hell are you?" His eyes suddenly opened wide. "Captain?"

I could not respond. The lump in my throat forbade it. I sat back quickly and looked away to the left, hiding my disfigurement.

"Is it really you? What in Kenny Rodger's beard happened to you?"

"Pilgrim," I stated blankly, refusing to look at him. He paused. Maybe for too long.

"Are you counter signing me?" He shifted, bringing his face closer to the bars. I could feel his eyes on me, taking in every grotesque detail he could see. When he had all he could take, he sat back. "Captain, what happened to you?"

"PILGRIM." I growled.

"Captain, how long has it been? I don't rememb—"

"PILGRIM, GOD DAMN IT!" My voice reverberated off the inside of our connected crates. My face turned slightly so I could see him. The only thing between us was a couple inches of steel bars and the plywood walls. I had to be sure.

Counter signing was a technique used on the battlefield to determine if the newly encountered troops were friendly or hostile. It was two simple predetermined words that all ally troops should know. One side would say the first word, the other side would respond with the other word. Then either relax or open fire. Our handler Sandy used to make up phrases with her intel spooks to hide the key words. She was forever going on about how it was preferable and more secure to use the words in a phrase, but we never did. In the field, when you happen upon troops you are not sure are friendly, you throw out a word. If they don't throw out the matching word, you throw lead. Simple. No time for anything else.

"Captain…I don't…" Postman hemmed and hawed. "STRIPES!" He blurted out. "No! Wait. That was in Iraq. DAMN IT…"

I started to reach through the bars.

"BOSTON!" He belted out. I froze.

"*Boston*… That's right. I got it. Postman delivers!" He sighed and chuckled quietly. "Boston. Yeah, nice place. The north end has some great food. Last time I was there, I left with a pasta hangover and a meatball the size of a hand-grenade." He smiled. "Hey, remember how Sandy used to make up those god damned stupid stories with the challenge words?" He giggled to himself. "Damn intel spooks. They could complicate a Happy Meal." His laugh was quick and higher pitched than his voice. It sounded like a giggle and I had forgotten how much I missed it.

"What is that?" I motioned to the Z-shaped scar on his left arm. He glanced at it and then looked at me with concern on his face. He scratched his ear almost nervously for a moment.

"It was a tattoo. You remember. A tattoo of a stamp."

"What was the picture on the stamp?" I pressed him. I needed to be absolutely sure. He stared at me scratching his ear. He looked surprised I was asking him these questions. But if he really was Postman, he would understand. And knowing him, he would be cheery about it.

"Really, it wasn't a stamp. It was a post mark. The post office uses an official mark, stamped on a letter with the place, date, and time of posting and serves to cancel the postage stamp. This postmark had a dog pile. A big dog pile of shit." He grinned. "Because I stamp more shit than a postman!" He giggled quoting the line that coined his nickname.

It was him.

I reached through the bars and grabbed his hand. I shook it like we used to.

"Damn, Postman! It is damn good to see you, old friend!" I smiled. He was a sight to see.

"You too! I thought you were dead. Hell, I thought the whole team was." He lowered his head. The single streak of moonlight caught his matted hair, and something looked funny. Not natural. I could only imagine what they did to him.

"What happened to the team?" he asked. "Do you know?"

I looked away and swallowed hard. Flashes of fire, pain and confusion ran through my head. I wished I could tell him, but honestly, I did not know. If I was really honest with myself, I wished they had all perished that day. A quick end was so much better than what I was going through every single day.

"I'm sorry. It's a blur. I only remember portions of it. Sometimes I see parts of it when I sleep, but never enough to know what happened to everyone. I think I might have been the first man down." I swallowed again and shook off the feelings of dread the questions were stirring up.

"What happened to your tattoo?" I asked. Postman shrugged.

"You know how these things go. They don't want us to be identifiable. No distinct markings. So, they removed my tats with a vegetable peeler." He spoke in a 'what are you going to do, that's life' kind of tone. Inwardly, I cringed at the thought.

"It could have been worse though. They could have done to me what they did to you." He moved closer to the bars again, his eyes studying my profile. "What the hell happened?"

I shrugged. "I don't know." I was keeping my head turned to the left, hiding the disgusting side of my face. I knew it could not hide it all, but it kept the worst parts concealed.

"You don't know? Or you don't want to know?" he asked.

"Does it matter?" I responded. "Either one leads to the beauty queen before you." I said sarcastically.

"Jesus. Not remembering might be a blessing, Cap," Postman said. "No offense, but that looks god damn painful. You look like a melted roll-on deodorant." He

116

giggled with that intoxicating energy. I could not help but smile. "Did they take your eye too? It looked like it was missing." I did not respond. "Cap…Cap?" I looked at him sideways refusing to face him. "Look at me, brother." He persisted. I shook my head slightly. He reached through the bars and grabbed my chin. Slowly he moved my head to face him. Slowly, not forcefully. I pushed his hand away.

"Don't ever be ashamed of the pain you have been through. It is a badge of honor. Raise your head up, Captain. This demands respect." He grinned at me, pointing to the left side of my face. "Suffering is what shapes us, makes us who we are. It makes us strong. It *forges* us. There is no growth without suffering." He leaned in. "My Mama used to tell this story. I thought it was stupid the first hundred times I heard it. But that was when I was young and foolish. I know better now.

"The story was about these clumps of dirt. She used to say they had feelings like people. One day, strong hands took the first clump of dirt, poured sticky, burning liquid on it, beat it, and squashed it flat. That first pile of dirt screamed in pain as it was churned and pounded and shaped. The other piles just looked on in horror. The first pile begged for help as it forever lost its dirtly shape. It begged for it all to stop. But the pain continued for a long, long time. Then, just when the first pile could take no more it was dropped into a thick container and thrown into the flames. The pain was even more unbearable, and the first pile screamed and begged for it to stop. But it did not. It stayed hot and intense until a long time later when that dirt pile was removed from the kiln, strong and solid. He emerged from the flames and tumbled from the container as a new heavy and strong brick. A brick that was the first cornerstone of a foundation that became a great, proud, strong building. Over time the other piles of dirt eroded and got carried away, piece by piece, on the wind to be lost forever. But long did that building stand. Long past all those piles and even the builders that made that first pile of dirt into that brick." He paused looking at me.

"You see, pain is strength. It's a simple and true formula. To be strong you have to endure the pain. There is no other way. But it is transformational pain. It is what you must go through to change and grow. Think about it. You see it is everywhere. To build muscle you must endure the pain of weight. To build mental strength you must endure the pain of suffering. And only that pain and strength can forge respect. That is what respect is. It is a man's wealth of pain." He scooted forward, closer to the bars.

"That is why the world is full of douchebags that get caught up in their own self-inflicted, dumbass problems. The only pain they know is what phone or trinket to buy next. But you…" He reached through the bars and took my chin again. "You are different. You have strength that shows. The strength of a leader. This…" He started to turn my face towards his. I pushed his hand away again. "This is pain that is beyond strength and respect." He paused not saying anything, waiting for me to respond. My hands shook as I fought back emotions. I had never thought of it the way he explained. Slowly, I turned to look at him exposing my full face.

"This is beautiful," he said. I smiled. The half of my mouth that worked showed my happiness. I suspected he was the only person in the world that could be optimistic enough to find beauty in the mess of this face.

"Does it hurt?"

I shrugged. "It feels funny to smile."

"Holy Hanukkah." He squinted, examining my face deeper. "Have they been using you as a punching bag too? How can you even speak? That lip looks…"

"My fault. I tried to escape." I almost chuckled.

"Escape? Christ. What the hell is wrong with you? I never even considered that. Security is god damned tight, and the drugs…" He rubbed his head. "It's hard to think. Hard to form thoughts. It's like high tide in my head. There are waves of random shit slamming into my consciousness, filling it with so much sludge, swirling around. It's so hard to think. It's damn near impossible to remember. I couldn't possibly plan anything. Even if I could, I would just god damn forget it two minutes later!" He cocked his head. "How did you do it? How far did you make it? Did you get out of your cell?"

"Heh. I was pretty close to free the last few times." I replied with a smirk.

"Few times!?" he choked in surprise.

"Almost to the blue door." I grinned proudly. "I was so close. The last attempt…I was out. I was in a truck driving away from this shit hole."

"Holy hell! You were driving away?" Postman shook his head "How the hell did you end up back here!?"

"I pulled over," I said.

"Whaaaat?" Postman giggled. It sounded like a joke, but once he saw my expression, he knew it wasn't.

"Wait. What?" he prodded, "To get drive thru? Seriously…why?"

"I caught my reflection for the first time." My voice was flat, hiding the deep pain. Postman's face went serious. "I hadn't seen what I had become before then," I said. "Not seen my face. Not seen my missing eye, hair, teeth, or ear. It cleared up a lot of things for me. Lack of depth perception. Being half deaf and blind…"

119

"So, big deal. You look like Gollum. He was a bad-ass. And you are the baddest ass I have ever met. And I have been to Harlem at night. You are biblically bad-ass!" Postman started his giggle.

"I don't want to be bad-ass," I said, the smile on my face faded back into the disfigurement. My voice just over a whisper, "I just want to go home. I don't want to do this anymore. I played my part. I did my job. I was good at it. I made a difference. I fought for those who could not. I gave so much of myself. So much of my innocence and morals. Can't we just stop this? Can't we just go home?" My voice faded into the darkness and plywood walls of the crates. Somewhere far off in the distance there was banging and shouting.

"Look, Cap…"

"There is no going home from this one." I cut my friend off. "No fat lady to sing. No happily ever after. Even if I could escape, I can't go back looking like this. I can't put my family in that situation. I am a monster now. Would you kiss this?" My hands were shaking, trembling in that strange spasmodic way.

"Don't talk like that."

"How *should* I talk?" I barked. "I have lived my life in the service of people that have left me behind! Abandoned me. Forgotten. I am all done. There is nothing left to give. Nothing left to press on for…"

"What!?" Postman leaned forward. For a long moment, his mouth moved but no words came out. "You can't be my Captain. That guy was one tough dude. You sit…"

"Cut the shit, Postman! You can't stoke my ego on this one. It is *gone*. This life is now valueless. There is nothing left for me. There is nothing here that I want anymore. There is nothing here that wants *me*!"

"How can you say that?" He fired back, his voice loud and strong. "What about your god damned family!? Are they valueless?"

"They are living a life in a place that has no room for what I have become! You said it yourself! They don't face this level of pain. They have a piece of shit truck and can barely deal with that! This is a far different level of suffering; I don't think they could ever be prepared to deal with!" I shouted back. "I don't fit in that world anymore! I'm not welcomed there!" My chest heaved. "You remember the V.A. hospital! How many times did we see it? HOW MANY TIMES!?" My voice boomed, reverberating through the connected crates. "Remember Rico!? He lost legs. She just dropped the ring on the bed and walked away without a word! THAT WAS JUST LEGS! LOOK AT ME! I would give both my legs to have my face back! You can hide legs, make it discreet, get a prosthetic… People can be nice. They can pretend they don't see. They can smile and be accepting for a limb. But a face… People cringe, they look away and hurry out of sight, not wanting to deal with you! It makes them sick!"

"But your family is different. That is not them, you don't know…"

"I DO!" I shouted over him. "They are wonderful and exceptional, but they are HUMAN! They can try to play the part, but humans are visual creatures. We chase shiny objects and seek out beauty. Instinctively we cover ourselves with shit that makes us look pretty and we collect shit that makes us feel beautiful." I swallowed, tasting the familiar distinct tin. Something was bleeding again, and it was pooling in my mouth. "No one ever collected anything that made them uglier. It is just not what humans do." I spat

121

the blood on the floor of the crate. My eyes dropped and I shook my head. "They are better off not knowing what happened. Their world is better off thinking I died a hero than knowing I became a monster."

"So that is it?" He fired back his voice tainted with anger. "So that is all? The great Captain Ross has finally given up. They finally beat you?"

"What did you say?" My voice was quiet and distant at first. Then, I lunged forward all at once pressing my face hard against the bars. Postman jumped back startled, glaring at me.

"I said 'DID THEY FINALLY BEAT YOU!?'" He howled back.

"No…not that..." I pressed harder against the bars without realizing it. I reached out to him. "What did you call me?" Postman looked at me shocked. He tugged at his ear as his eyes went wide. My own fingers twisted and contorted into strange spasmatic shapes as my mind reeled through the haze.

"Captain…" his voice cautious. "Are you asking me…your name?" His expression was incredulous. He raised one eyebrow as if he were trying to figure out if I was joking. But when his eyes met my one blue, hungry, tortured eye, he knew, and responded.

"Captain…Ross."

"That's…that's…" I stuttered and shook like a wino pulling myself up to the bar after days of sobriety. "That's my name?" I asked, my voice a raspy whisper. In my head I was trying it on. Trying to picture people calling me Ross. Trying to recall how it sounded, how it felt.

"Cap?" Postman asked, his voice soft now. "You alright?" He shifted forward. "You didn't know your own name? How in the hinges of hell did you not know your own name? Cap?"

"Is that my last name?" I asked.

"Man, what did they do to you?"

"First name?" My voice was laced with a hint of begging. A wino for knowledge.

"Last. Last name." Then he paused for only a moment before saying,

"Captain David Ross."

"That's right!" I said joyfully. "Son of a bitch! That's right!" It fits. I could feel it. It felt like me. I could hear the name now, over and over from many different people at many different times. I was a boy, I was a man, I was in school, people called me David, they called me Ross. I had a name. How could it be that I did not know this? How could I have forgotten? A tear left my eye.

"Man, are you alright? How could you not have known? What do they call you?"

I laughed the smallest of laughs. I felt like a child on Christmas after just opening a grand present, like a starving man thrown a loaf of bread. I wiped quickly at my cheek.

"Bastard," I replied. "That might be the nicest thing they call me." I chuckled quietly. "When they are not calling me that, they call me Captain. Or seven-one-five," I said, my mind still reeling with so many things suddenly falling into place, memories blossoming.

"Whoa, whoa, whoa…" Postman said raising his hands. His eyes were wide. "YOU are seven one five? *YOU?*" He pointed "Holy Snoopy shit! OF COURSE!"

"What are you talking about?" My forehead wrinkled in confusion. I wiped my face again.

"Seven-one-five. I thought he was a mental patient here. Man, the stories I have overheard from the guards!" His eyes lit up. "Wait, wait, wait! I have to know!" He was suddenly all amped up now. "Is it true you made a bomb out of shit!?"

I grinned, the undamaged half of my face lighting up. "Combustible gasses…"

"OH, MY FUCKING GOD!" He howled in laughter. "Did you immobilize two guards at the same time by handcuffing them together and then putting a stun gun to the cuffs? Did I hear that right?" I smiled again, and he roared with laughter.

"Actually, I was not the one holding the stun gun, I made another guard do that." I told him as he laughed his high-pitched giggle.

"You jumped out your fucking window? There is no way *that* is true!"

"Yeah," I replied. "But that did not work out the way I planned," I said regretfully. He howled in laughter. For several long moments it was like it was before and I almost felt happy.

"Brother, you jumped out a fucking fourth story window! No shit it did not work out the way you planned!" Postman giggled, then he squinted, a look of curiosity crossed his face.

"But wait. I have also heard them say you have never killed any of the guards. You have had chances, lots of them, but you never did. True?"

"True."

"Really? How? Why?"

"They are just soldiers. They are following orders. They are not the real enemy," I began. "You know, I have heard stories of men meeting in the trenches of World War Two. Both trying their best to kill each other. Years after the war, they meet again and become quite good friends. Soldiers are people too. Humans even." I smiled crookedly. "They have lives, families, and loved ones when they leave here. They are following orders. If it were up to them, they would not hold us here. I believe that. They are just following orders. I would not rob them of their lives or families." I swallowed hard. "Not to mention there is kind of a balance. An unspoken agreement. If I kill one of them, then I truly believe they would kill me."

"What the hell? That is what they are doing to us!" Postman interjected. "Robbing us of our lives! Our families!"

"Look, I would not wish this life on anybody. Even my enemy," I responded. Postman just stared at me, pulling on his ear with his mouth open, unable to find words. As usual, it did not take him long.

"Dude, they are holding us hostage and torturing us." He giggled sarcastically. "That makes no sense."

"Does not change my opinion. I know, from the bottom of my soul, I don't want anyone or anyone's family to go through what I am going through or what my family is going through." I said flatly, my voice unwavering.

Postman looked down and shook his head ever so slightly and sighed.

"You are a better man than I am," he said lowly. The way he said it, I was not even sure he was talking to me.

"So, what are the plans for your next escape? I'm in cell 612, right across the hall from this god damned room. We are in sector six now. Your cell is in sector seven, the seriously secure sector. Your next escape, don't leave without me," he giggled. I stared at him blankly. I was not sure what to say. I knew the truth. I understood why. But would he? I doubted it.

"There's no next escape." I dropped my head.

"What? Why? What do you mean?" He questioned. "If you can make it that far by yourself, god damn, I am sure we can make it with both of us!"

I did not look up. I did not respond.

"Come on man, you hoard data! You always know just the right way to expose a weakness."

I did not respond. The long pause suddenly exposed the weight in the air.

"Wait…." Postman began to figure it out. "What are you talking about? I know you! You always have a…" He trailed off as he stared at me, his eyes narrowing. Here it comes. "You are not really serious…are you?"

"What do I have to return to? There is nothing left for me." I asked.

"So—you are just going to die here?"

I said nothing.

"Wait…" It all started coming together for him. It took so long for him because he was such an optimist. For him, everything would eventually all be better. He could never consider such a thing. It just was not in his way of thinking. He never reached those truly deep, dark corners of the soul.

"So—the easy way out!? Suicide is a better option?" He raised his voice. I did not respond. The silence answered louder than I ever could. "You're fucking kidding me!"

"I am a broken man!" I finally roared.

"How does that make you different from any other god damned person walking this planet?" He fired back, anger in his tone. "We are all broken. Everyone one of us! Some inside, some outside. But we are all fragmented. Yours just shows. Yours is a pain we can see, and it is *beautiful*! Don't let anyone tell you different!" He jabbed a finger at me, "Because if you hide and cower and cover it up, then and only then, does it become a weakness! It will become sick and ugly. Like some huge wart." His voice rang out and cut me off from rebutting.

"If you walk around with your head held high, showing what makes you strong and different, then people will not be disgusted, they will be curious, they will be inspired, they will want to understand your pain, understand your suffering and strength. They will understand and respect. They will accept you! They will want to know how you went through it all and were strong enough to hold your head up! They will want to know your story! They will want to be you!"

"But…" I interrupted. He kept on talking over me.

"There ain't no fucking buts!" He was shouting now. His eyes were fierce and he spit as he barked at me.

"You always told the team that every person was different, every person had something unique to offer, every person had found his or her place in the team not because the team member was like the next person, but because each one was different, with different strengths in different areas! That is what makes a team! God damn it, you have strength! It's a new and different strength, but it is a strength! A strength not only for this team, but for everyone. This is what the world needs. Strong people to stand up and be proud to show personal pain. Maybe it will inspire people to rediscover real values! Maybe it will teach them what real respect is!"

"But my family, I can't—"

"Bullshit!" He cut me off. "BULL. FUCKING. SHIT." He punched the floor. "Who the hell told you it was your choice!? Who told you that?" His chest was heaving. He punched downward again as he scolded me. "You have no right to choose for them! You want to do something for them? Prepare yourself for their worst reaction and then let them decide whether they love you, or your god damned face!" He wiped his mouth and paused. I could hear footsteps echoing beyond our crates.

"Flip the scenario." He said trying to regain his composure. "Would you want a body bag or a chance to have a father? A wooden box or a wife?" He shook his head. "Think of it from your kid's point of view! I know as a child what I would want! Even damaged, even mangled, I know what I would choose." He punched the wall and the two connected crates shuttered. "IT IS NOT YOUR GOD DAMNED CHOICE!" His voice cracked. "I never had a father. But I would have taken the ugliest mother fucker from the ugliest mother fucking land over what I had." His head dropped and he slumped. "Be strong! Be the cornerstone in their foundation! Be strong. Be what they can build on!" He wiped his face. "You have no right to choose for them." His eyes were ablaze with outrage as they met mine.

"So, don't."

There was no counter argument. He was right. My father was a bastard. I never looked at him as ugly or handsome, damaged or whole. To be honest, I would have to think about it just to decide. Same with my mother. Sure, she was always beautiful to me, but that is through the eyes of a child, through the lens of love. It made you see things differently. Like the way my grandparents were so in love. They stole kisses like teenagers when no one was looking. Two people, late in life, youth and beauty gone. Yet they saw each other as gorgeous and irresistible.

This is what love does. It changes how you see things. That was its incredible power. I had forgotten. This dark, hot, sand-filled hole had robbed me of it.

I looked at Postman. Reaching through the bars I put a hand on his shoulder. He flinched, then looked at it like it was the first time a touch was not intended to harm him in a full lifetime. I guess it was I who did not understand, not him. He looked back at me with the eyes of an abused dog.

"So, you will do it? Stick it out? Let them decide?" he asked.

"I just…I don't know how this is all going to turn out…" I hemmed. "What do you say? I mean, when it all goes south and they decide… How do you leave, knowing you are never coming back…? What could you possibly say…?"

"The only thing that needs to be said." Postman's voice was low and firm. "Tell them everything will be alright." I looked at him.

"I don't want to hurt them or place them in a situation that…"

"Do what Fisher-Price would have done," Postman said.

Fisher-Price?

Oh, just the name brought the memories flooding back. Fisher-Price was the last member to join the team. He was young and his real name was Julio. But he was brilliant, imaginative and a huge fan of the plastic brick building kits called Legos. This was how he got the call sign.

"Fisher-Price would always start out with those Legos and plans to build a car or house. But damn, shit would change and he would end up building a robot or spend thirty-eight days building a god damned life size yeti. Remember that thing? That man would start with a plan and let opportunity dictate where he ended up. That grown man made some incredible shit out of toy blocks." Postman shook his head in respect.

"Captain, that is what you need to do. Not the Legos, but the plan. Make a plan for them to reject you. I know that is hard to hear, but it is not as grim as the long dirt nap. What if there is a chance? That is a mistake you can't fix. Get your mind right and make your plans. Line up an apartment, job, everything in a different city if you have to. Then, when it's all set up, go to them. Be prepared for this to be your goodbye. Then talk to them. Let them make the choice. If your plan is set and mind is right to go it alone, there is nothing to lose. It will all go down just like you planned. Say goodbye. Enjoy them one last time. But let them choose, and if they want you, you tear that plan up in that different city and you make a new plan. Together.

"Together, build a yeti." He said finally.

I dropped my head. I don't remember Postman ever being this wise, but he was right. I was halfway there. Considering suicide, I thought I would never see them again. This would at least give me one last moment with them. Worst case, I could always do it after they rejected me. Maybe that is my new plan. Delay my current plan and allow things to play out at home. At the very least, I could see them one last time.

"I just don't know if I could handle their rejection. I'm not sure I can prepare for that," I told him.

"Just give it some time. Think on it," he said. I did not respond. A hundred scenarios raced through my head. I just did not know.

The footsteps were growing louder. We were running out of time.

"Hey," I said. "Where, the hell, are we?"

"In crates. Packed up like some god damned special delivery." Postman chuckled for a moment. "Some god damned hospital, in some god damned desert," he replied more seriously.

"Hospital?" I questioned, "Like what we did to…"

"That was not us. We followed orders. We dropped him off there in the ER. It was the military doctors who took them from there… We just followed the orders…" Postman suddenly stopped talking and cocked his head. It was obvious. It just occurred to him what I was talking about earlier. Just soldiers following orders. We would never have done that.

"Ironic," I said.

"Not really. The world copies great ideas. I bet the U.S. did not even come up with the medicinal prison. I bet we just god damned perfected it."

"I meant that we would end up in one," I said.

"I know what you really meant," Postman said, then closed his mouth and nodded. He was right. There were no words.

"Do you know which desert we are in? Which country? When the Humvee blew up, we were in Pakistan…"

"Nope. Do you recognize the uniforms patches?" he asked.

"No. I have spent a lot of time staring at them, but I can't place it." He nodded, pulling on his ear.

"Why are we in these crates?" I asked hurriedly.

"They usually put me in one of these when they are working on the cell. When they put the steel bars outside the windows, I was in one of these for a few hours," Postman recalled.

"So, they must be doing something to both of our cells if they have us out at the same time and put in here together. I wonder what is waiting for us."

"Hopefully it's the new big screen TV!" Postman laughed.

"Dr. Idnkel! Have you come across Dr. Idnkel?" I asked.

"Who?" Postman sat up and pulled at his ear. "Who the hell is that?"

"I was hoping you could tell me. I need more intel. I think he is the bearded bastard who has been interrogating me."

"Wait," Postman said. "The bearded guy? Looks like a spec ops soldier?"

"Yes! What do you know? Where can I find this fucker?" I sat up straight grabbing the bars. "Who is he? This guy is the key, with him, we can…"

A door burst open and light poured in blinding us both. Shouting filled the air and our crates were pulled away from each other. Suddenly pointed sticks were thrust through the bars jabbing and sticking us with needles. I reached out to my old friend as we collapsed to the bottom of each create and the world spun into the murky depths of our medicinal prison.

12. A MAN WITH A PLAN

It started as a distant discomfort. Suddenly, it was sharp and crushing.

I tried to pull my fingers away, but something pinned my hand down. A watering eye shot open just in time to catch the blurred kick to my ribs. I coughed unintentionally. The air was forced from my lungs. A large figure loomed over me. He stood scowling down at me with one of his boots standing on my left hand. He grinned, then repeatedly kicked my ribs with his other steel-toed boot. I twisted and shifted trying to do anything to soften the blows, but the restraints held me mostly in place. He kicked until he was breathing hard.

"Oh…" He panted before saying sarcastically in mock surprise, "Are you awake?" In his hand was a food tray. He looked at it, and then back at me. "Breakfast!" he exclaimed in a gasping sing-song tone. Then rotated his wrist, dumping the contents of the tray onto the dusty concrete floor.

Got it.

I recognized this man.

The square jaw was the giveaway. This was the security lead from Jabba's skiff. Funny, he looked much happier now than the first time I saw him. Of course, at that time, he was keeled over, holding his groin in pain.

Without another word he spat in the splatter of food on the floor and turned to take his exit. He rotated, grinding his boot into my fingers, filling my morning with a fresh dose of pain. Slowly and carefully, he treaded through the food and exited the room.

My eyes blinked the bright light away. It was not direct sunlight, but it was still golden bright and I cursed it. How could it be? How could something so warm and inviting exist when my whole world was in ruins. It mocked me and I cursed it.

I looked around and took in the familiar sight of my dingy cell. The smell stung my nose. A new layer of construction dust covered everything. The shackles on my left wrists and ankles caught my attention. I sighed. Another day begins. This was a new thing. They unshackled one side and allowed me to undo the other side when I awoke. I could move around and use the toilet. I guess it was a way to keep me in place just long enough to swap out food or hose down the cell.

Before, they would have me put my hands through the sliding slat in the door where they would handcuff me. That was before that one time when in a single quick motion, I managed to make the guard handcuff himself to me. I then pulled his arm repeatedly, and violently through the slat until he collapsed unconscious, and I ended up riding another needle to La-La Land.

I freed myself from the shackles and sat up. The crusted and rusty springs of the thin, flat mattress creaked with my movement. Some of the springs poked through the bottom and scraped the concrete floor as I moved. I closed and opened my left hand repeatedly. It was already bruising in the patten of his boot print. Nothing broken though. What a dick.

Another fucking day. I sighed.

What day was it? How long was I in that crate? I felt particularly rested, so I was not sure how many days I had slept.

There was a positive. I felt like I was healing. The bruises on my face and body were transitioning from that deep red and purple to brown and yellow. They entered that stage where they began to itch. My teeth seemed to be tightening back up and no longer clicked back and forth as I bit down. The injuries to my fingers, knuckles, shoulder, and well, most joints had transformed from pain to stiffness. My nose though, that still hurt like hell. I could not breathe through it and the slightest sneeze or touch made my eyes water and brought new and creative curses to my discolored lips.

Suddenly, something new caught my eye.

Where the dark, heavy, steel door had been, was now a four-inch-thick, ballistic glass entryway. A door constructed entirely of bullet-resistant glass that allowed every Tom, Dick, and Harry that walked by a full view into my glamorous life. It seems I am to be kept under constant supervision. The only privacy I was allowed now was the single narrow wall that just barely cut off the view to my john.

However, even that was on the renovation list. Blue chalk lines traced the narrow wall seams where it met the floor and ceiling. It seems that was to be removed. Soon, there would be nowhere to hide.

I guess that last escape attempt really pissed them off.

Postman's words came rushing back to me, then the full events of our encounter. I remembered our conversation and his words rung through my mind all at once. He was right. There were "upgrades" to my prison. It was great to see him again. To talk and just be in his presence. It was a brief departure from this hell. In fact, it was so enjoyable I can't even remember what I was doing bef—

A wave of panic flooded me.

The phone!

The cell phone I stole back from these assholes... Where did I leave it!? Wait...I was carving out a hiding place for it...I slipped off the toilet and knocked myself unconscious.

I left it on the toilet!

My wide eye shot to the hopper and met a strange shape. It was not my phone, but what looked like...what the...? It almost looked like papers. Folded and organized. Not just any papers though...

Were those...blueprints?

HOLY.

SHIT.

I froze. As much as I wanted to leap over there and grab it, I knew I could not. I had to ensure I would not be caught with that stuff. I had to be careful now that everyone could constantly see me. If I jumped up and huddled in the corner unfolding a large paper, every soldier in this hemisphere would be in here clubbing me like a seal. I needed to ensure I could spend some time with it and memorize it before they found it. And they would find it, so I needed to be prepared to best utilize my time with it.

My gaze instantly fixed on the clear door. I watched the people move by. Soldier. Sentry. Officer. Some asshole. Woman with cup. Guard. Soldier. I studied the traffic patterns. A sentry passed by regularly traveling from left to right. I could tell it was a sentry because of the consistency.

Others passed by at random. They tended to be engrossed in other things and seldom looked in after the first pass by. It seemed once they saw the new door, they seemed less enthusiastic about seeing what lay beyond the fancy new entry way. The sentries though, they glared every time and they kept walking by, over and over and over.

It took a few hours, but I figured out the rhythm. The sentry guards swapped out about once per hour. They had a patrol that took them roughly seventy-one seconds to complete. The current guard, a dark haired, dark skinned man with a gray streak in his beard that started from under his lower lip, took eighty-four seconds. I nicknamed him Gruel, as the gray streak in his beard made him look like he was drooling gruel. Anyway, when a female passed by, intersecting his path, he took no less than ninety-six seconds and up to one hundred and forty-four seconds. Funny thing was, it did not matter what the female looked like, it would always delay him. Gruel carried a silver Zippo lighter. He flipped it open and closed constantly. *Click*, open. *Cluk*, closed. *Click-cluk*. He strode up and down the hall like he owned the place. *Click-cluk, click-cluk.*

Just as he passed out of sight this last time, I darted to the toilet. I grabbed the folded blueprints and a thin black square clattered to the floor.

"Holy shit!" Unable to hold my excitement. I could not believe my luck. The phone was still here! Not only that, someone had left building blueprints on top of it. Almost like one of the goons working on the door, mistook *this* phone for his boss's phone and returned the plans to the wrong friggin' phone!

"Holy shit!" I said unfolding the unique paper. It was blueprints. In fact, it was the prints for the building. Not the complete prints, but this floor and the one below it.

They must have been tracing water and electrical lines to make sure they did not damage any during their construction. "So what?" you say. "Big deal?" you say. This *is* a big deal. It looked like right behind the main security desk on this floor, there was a hallway that led almost directly to the security room in the parking garage. Then, I noticed something. Whoa. I took in every line on the huge paper, my eyes hungry for information. I had located a main cluster of cable. It was in the same spot on both floors. I studied the prints, lining them up. This meant that somewhere below, all these cables lead to one main panel.

Interesting.

A new exfiltration strategy started to form in my mind. Images, ideas, options, and responses flooded my swirling head. This had real possibilities. Not only do I have a plan and route now, but I have a way to predict what these fuckers would do. And if I know what they are going to do, I can use that against them. This gave me just enough to form a plan that would confuse the entire infrastructure and produce enough chaos that my chances of escape where not based on mere desperation and hope.

This might actually work.

For an instant I thought of my family. For an instant, I was not half a world away. I was caressing her thick, dark hair and his little fingers grabbed for my own. I looked at the phone and my heart sunk. I blinked my one good eye several times as my mind ground to a halt.

I touched the left side of my face.

I can't do this to them.

I just can't.

Echoes in my memory repeated Postman's words. "It's not your choice!" I heard his voice. But really, what does he know? Everything will always come up roses through his eyes. He was a die hard, unrealistic optimist.

"It's not your choice!"

He is not me, I told myself. He has never faced a situation like this.

"It's not your choice!"

Damn it, Postman. There is no way they could be happy with me in their lives. It just does not add up. I refuse to be their burden.

"It's not your choice!"

I realized I had lost count. The sentry could be by at any second. I folded the blueprints back up and hurried to the mattress. Leaping on it, I slid the prints under it. I was just about to slide the phone under as well when I paused.

"A body bag or a father?"

Fucking Postman. I am going to break him out of his cell just to kick the shit out of him. This has nothing to do with him. How dare he put these thoughts in my head! I was fine. My path laid out. I had a plan. It made sense. Sure, it had collateral damage, but it was only me and it benefitted far more than it cost. He had no fucking right!

I looked over at the food splattered onto the floor with spit and two boot prints in it. I smiled. I could laugh because I had no plan to eat. Ever again. You see, my fundamental problem was ironic. Really ironic. It seemed that my driving sense of survival was a double-edged sword. As hard as I had ever fought to escape and prevail now spun on me as I tried to execute my latest plan.

It was not complicated. A child could pull it off. It was not even possible for these assholes to stop it when executed properly. It just required something I seem to have a real problem doing. It has made me realize something I never thought I could say about myself.

I am a coward.

I can't do it. I have killed countless others, but I cannot kill myself. I know, I tried. The sharpened spring to the wrists, the makeshift noose fastened from shoestrings and then again months later assembled from pants. Even a few good cracks of my skull against the concrete wall. How about a graceful swan dive onto the floor from the top of the toilet? Even that might do it. All those plans will work with proper execution. However, they were all performed half-heartedly. If I could have performed them with the same determination I used on the battlefield, or in escape, I would have been in a box long ago.

I subtly looked over my shoulder, watching the glass entryway. Outside the door, Gruel finally strode by. He eyed my back to him, slumped in defeat. He glared, flipping his lighter open and closed, *click-cluk*, *click-cluk*. His sight only left me when he took the time to smile at a passing woman. How the hell did he even see her? This guy must have a sixth sense. Like Perv-Power or something.

I looked back at the food on the floor and returned to my thoughts. I find it ironic that I never feared battle, death, or any enemy. I charged full speed and head-first into conflicts, life-and-death situations, wars, and firefights. I never hesitated or even considered what would or even could happen to me. But this…THIS…I can't do. I just can't bring myself to follow through. I cannot even explain why.

I have no will to live, yet no courage to die.

I see now why a gun is so welcoming in this situation. A single moment of weakness. One single fully committed decision and it is done. As asshole Brian would say, "a moment of clarity." A second would be all it would take. Just the briefest of moments. Each of my attempts began with that one fully committed, clear moment. But time… Time robs that commitment, it taints thoughts with regret and second guesses, and before I knew it, I had lost the nerve.

I have never fought a battle that was so difficult. Never faced an enemy so strong. I have never been so grossly outmatched.

I looked down at the phone.

"Fuck you!" I cursed Postman, wherever he was.

I tore the seam of the mattress and folded the building plans into a small square that fit through the tear. I should not need these plans or the knowledge from them.

Before I executed any of these plans, there were things I had to figure out first. And I think I knew how to do it.

In the new layer of construction dust on the floor next to the new tear in my mattress, I drew out a grid. It was barely visible but just enough for me to see. I filled the top row with the alphabet followed by the numbers zero through nine. I would need to crack this and memorize it before the grid was cleaned or was discovered, so time was short. But not because of the cleaning.

Keeping my slumped back facing the new ballistic glass door, I powered up the cell phone. After a moment her gorgeous picture appeared beneath a web of splintered glass. I was prompted for a password and presented a grid of strange symbols. Starting from the top left, I copied the symbol under the number one in the dust grid, then number two and so on.

A moment later I hid the phone under the mattress and moved to the barred window, fixing my gaze far off in the distance. About nineteen seconds later than expected, I saw the reflection of Gruel striding by, his eyes burning into my back. As he moved past the door and out of sight, I returned to the mattress and pulled out the phone. This was going to have to be my process.

Seventy second work cycles.

I finished filling the odd numbers into the grid and stared at it in the dust. The numbers I knew on the top row, their odd shaped 'numbers' below. Software companies don't rearrange the location of the numbers, they just change the language or font for them. The location of each shape gave away what number it really was. I now had a cipher for their numbers. I just needed to figure out the passcode to unlock the damn phone and I could do the same for the keyboard.

I searched my memory in every manner I could think of. Long and hard I thought. I tried to picture myself typing in numbers. I tried to pick the phone up quick and punch in the unlock code to test for muscle memory. Nothing. For hours I struggled to recall what it could be, every seventy seconds taking my place at the window. Could it be a partial phone number? A date? Military code? Pattern?

Brian arrived two hours later, and his goons strapped me back down. We went through the same fucking questions, giving the same bullshit answers. I stopped answering just about the time someone came in and whispered into his ear. They rushed out freeing only my right hand. I could not free my other appendages in time to catch any of them before they left out my fancy new door.

Over the next several days I worked on the phone in seventy second work cycles. I tried everything. Every obvious number combination I could think of. I would make a list of them, fire up the phone punch them all in, swear and rage, then shut down the phone and start on a new list.

I began thinking I was never going to get this number when it suddenly occurred to me.

I tipped the phone and peered across it sideways so I could see every piece of crusted shit that was stuck on the shattered screen. There, clear as day, were two bloody fingerprints. Not smears or smudges, but nice blood-hardened prints that displayed round finger outline complete with clear prints. I smiled a melted and twisted lopsided grin. If you have ever been fingerprinted, you will know that it starts in a certain way, with a clean downward motion. A downward pressing motion. Like pressing a button.

Or typing on a number pad.

I moved my one good eye closer.

Holy.

Zombie.

Jesus.

It was not two bloody fingerprints. It was four! Each fingerprint had a jagged outline shifted just off center, like it was pressed twice. This means the code was a combination of only two digits. My heart was pounding in my chest so hard that I could feel it in my right ear.

146

I turned the phone back on and stared in awe.

The fingerprints were positioned above the number one and number two buttons. My hands began to shake and move in strange spasmodic rhythms. Somewhere in the caverns of my mind a melody echoed from the depths. A tear or sweat crossed my cheek and tumbled through the air, splashing down into the filth of the floor. My breathing was labored and came in heavy breaths as I ran number combinations through my head, searching for a familiar feeling…

Then I stopped.

I swallowed and forced myself to breathe. All air seemed to have left the room as if it were suddenly a vacuum.

I knew the passcode.

13. MAN DOWN

My stare was as empty as my mind.

It appeared like I was gazing out the window, but I was not. Night had fallen and the sandy horizon was overcome by blackness. The new glass cell door behind me let in more light than before. This transformed the window's view of the dark, empty, desert night into a mirror.

I stared at the shirtless body reflecting back at me. The image was so shocking it seized my mind. Mangled, melted, twisted, and discolored, I was a wreck of a human. What was not warped and burned was textured with old bruises, scrapes, and deep cuts. It tainted the contour of a once manly and pleasing face. Scars and missing pieces made up the landscape of my physique. New purple flourishes bloomed on my bony left ribcage. The steel toed boots from this morning almost recognizable beneath the tapestry of scars, welts, and heat-distorted skin. She used to run her fingers gently down my face, across my chest. She used to use words like "handsome" and "gorgeous."

Those words no longer fit.

For the first time in hours, I tore my eyes away, looking unintentionally up. There was a small gap in the drywall surrounding the back side of the light fixture. In that gap hid my cell phone. I knew how to unlock it. I knew the code. But I could not bring myself to use it. Why? My eyes fell to the reflection in the window again.

That's why.

I was damaged goods. Defective property. There would never again be a home sweet home for me. Every fiber of my being wanted to flush that phone down the toilet.

Why was I even wrestling with this? It was stupid.

Because of Postman. Because of his words. I would never even consider this, if not for what he said. If it had been anyone else, I could have thrown such a preposterous idea aside without a second thought. But it was him. It was the passion in his words.

In the window's reflection I saw Gruel pass by, outside my door. He glared in at me flipping that damned lighter, *click-cluk*. It had been a long day for him. Really long. They usually swapped sentries every hour, but I had noticed him outside my shiny new door this morning. I wondered briefly if he was being punished, or was he doing someone a favor by covering a few shifts? It was dangerous to think of him this way. To think of him as human. To think of any of them that way.

Enough distractions. I was either going to do this or not.

Decide soldier.

As Gruel disappeared out of sight, I began counting down from seventy seconds. I looked up at the light fixture and took a deep breath. Then, I retrieved the phone and powered it up. The screen blinked to life. After a moment of being lost in her beauty, I poked the screen. The unlock screen took over, brandishing a number pad.

Moment of truth.

One, two, two, one.

Twelve twenty-one.

December 21st.

His birthday.

I punched it in and the number pad vanished. The main screen appeared. The background was a picture of a baby grinning wide, with huge snowman double dimples. I smiled. How could you not?

I could not read the titles, but I knew what the icon looked like. A roundish blue icon with a word bubble in it. The text messaging application. There it was. I poked it.

Nothing.

I poked it again.

Nothing.

"What the…?" Wait…the shattered screen. I poked the edge of the icon, where there was an undamaged triangle of glass, and suddenly the screen changed. A list of conversations appeared. Names of people I had been messaging, with the top being the last conversation before the ambush. But that conversation was different. Each other conversation listed below, was labeled with letters, names. Instead of a name in the top conversation, I had somehow entered a picture. A small photo of a ball and chain.

"Damn it! What an asshole!" I cursed out loud before I could stop myself. Sometimes I was just the ultimate moron. Why couldn't I just have used her name! Is that so hard?

"Shit!" I hissed with gritted teeth. This is something that is very difficult for me. It has haunted me and made me sick since it happened. It keeps me up at night and at times I feel it on the tip of my tongue, but I just can't recall. As hard as I try…

I can't remember her name.

I was really hoping to see it here. Something so stupid and insignificant, but so important. I needed to know. I am humiliated and embarrassed. I am not sure how, but I just can't recall it. The love of my life, yet I don't know her name. What kind of person does that make me? I can recollect every detail of her eyes, her face, her body. Every word she ever said to me. But why could I not remember her name!? It was disheartening and made me feel so stupid. I looked at the tiny image, entered as a joke, as if I did not have a care in the world at that moment. It mocked me, and, in that instant, I hated myself.

I poked the "Ball and Chain" conversation and then stuffed the phone down my pants as I counted down with only four seconds left. Then, I waited for the sentry to pass by. Fifty, yes fifty seconds later, Gruel strode by, his eyes scanning my room, a bullshit grin on his face. This guy just rubbed me the wrong way. What the hell was the delay? This is the kind of soldier that gets guys killed. As he moved out of sight, I started counting down again and withdrew the phone.

What do I say?

Damnit. I didn't think of that.

I have no idea what to say. What's ironic is, I would know exactly what to say if I was saying goodbye. If I knew I would never see them again. It was so easy.

'It will be alright.'

Simple, encouraging and to the point. Maybe it is a soldier thing. It's easier to say goodbye then hello. However, let's not oversimplify it. This was not just your standard hello. This was, much more. What do you say to someone who thinks you are dead? It is not an easy subject to approach.

I can't waste time thinking this over or I would talk myself out of it. Time to wing it. I touched the text area and it brought up the keyboard.

Shit.

I forgot I had not done this yet. I needed to decode the letters. It was not hard, but it would take a little time. I could use the keyboard layout to do it. I made my way over to the dusty corner and filled in the letter cypher I had prepared on the dirty floor. Every seventy seconds I hid the phone and stared into my gruesome reflection until Gruel passed by. About forty minutes later a new sentry appeared. He was young. Looked tough. He was clearly scared.

With the cypher finally in place I brought up the screen and began to hunt and peck the keyboard using the cypher to spell out what I wanted to say. I got about thirty letters in, when I realized only nine letters had appeared.

Damn.

The broken screen was not registering properly. I would have been pissed, but the damn phone *had* been through an explosion. And while it was shattered, slightly twisted and bent, it was still in better shape than I was.

OK. I have an idea. Next to the thin text line that held exactly nine letters was a round button with the silhouette of a microphone. I touched it. The screen changed and the phone vibrated in my hand.

"Hello?" I said quietly and letters appeared in the text bar.

"Ohhh shit!" I said excitedly. More letters appeared. No, no, no! I clicked on and deleted all the letters.

This could work. I pressed the microphone button and began to dictate.

"I am OK," I said as quietly as possible, "But I need help." Letters appeared. My heart raced, pounding in my chest. I crouched back down and compared the letters to what I expected using the cypher. Here is what it read:

"I am Moe Kay. Buttery help."

You have got to be kidding me. That's not even close. OK, let me try again, I think I might just need to adjust my speech. I deleted all the letters and hit the microphone button again.

"I…am…OK" I said. The screen paused then letters appeared. I quickly decoded. These were spot on. Alright. I just needed to speak slowly and clearly with an even tone. I can do this.

I pressed the button again and said, "But I need help." I checked the letters.

"But guy need help."

Ha! At least it is getting closer. So, yeah. Slow and clear, speak slow and clear. I was so excited I had forgotten already. "But…I…need…help" I said, then hurriedly checked the letters. Perfect.

I hit the Send button without hesitation and then realized the weight of what I had just done. Typical. I had a history of acting without thinking. Often, this is what got me into trouble. I could hear my heartbeat in my ear and my hands began to shake. A distant rhythm played somewhere off in the echoes of my mind.

Three dots appeared below the bubble of my text. A distant *click-cluk, click-cluk* caught my ears. Shit! I jammed the phone down my pants. With all the excitement I had lost count. I felt the phone vibrate but I did not move and I kept my gaze fixed on the reflection in the window.

Every second I stood there at that window, waiting for the sentry, was an eternity. What did the message say?

Was it her? Would she be happy? Would she be upset? My mind raced. Is it hot in here? I was sweating profusely and my whole body shook like that torturous winter beach training back in BUD/S.

What was I doing? This was stupid. Damn it, Postman.

A *tap, tap, tap* on my door brought me back to reality. Slowly, I pulled my gaze off the window and looked over my shoulder. Outside my glass door, staring in, were two men. The one on the right was a new young guard. The one on the left was Gruel tapping my door with the fucking lighter. He grinned, then flipped me the bird. I chuckled slightly as they roared with laughter, pointing and laughing. Eventually, they backed away. Assholes. With a *click-cluk, click-cluk*, Gruel led his new recruit down the hall on their sentry and I began counting down once again.

I took a deep breath and removed the phone. It took me several seconds to build up the courage to look. There on the lock screen was a message. Her reply. I decoded it as fast as humanly possible. Short and to the point.

"Wrong number."

Wait. What?

I unlocked the phone and started to dictate. It took some time to confirm each letter of the text. After four countdowns and flybys by Gruel and his lacky, I finally sent the message.

"This is the right number. You know who I am. This is an open line so I can't use names."

Two more countdowns and one more finger. Finally, her response came in. After decoding it, this was what she said:

"How did you get this number? Who the hell is this?"

Ugh. I can feel it already. She is going full-Italian on me. DEFKON 3.

"You know who this is. They told you I was killed, but I survived. I am being held by the enemy. POW."

Nine countdowns and no response. I think I scared her away. Worse, I feared I was wasting the precious battery charge. I started to think I should just shut the phone off and try again in the morning. I will spend some time thinking about exactly the right thing to say. Then suddenly three dots appeared beneath my last text. She was typing. Half a world away, at this very moment in time, our lives were aligned. She was responding to me. It had been so long. A few seconds later, a message appeared. I deciphered it as fast as I could:

"I just called the CO. He is coming with the MPs to pick up this phone. They will trace this. They will find you. This is not funny."

I was elated. She called my Commanding Officer and the Military Police. DEFKON actually worked to my advantage for once. This was going better than I thought! I dictated and validated the texts between countdowns. I hurried, soon it would be time for them to come strap me down and medicate me up. The night was growing long, and the moon slowly inched across the sky. Here are the messages we exchanged:

"You called Pat? That's my girl. Tell him to triangulate the signal from this phone. I don't know where I am other than a hospital in some desert. Tell him medicinal prison. He will understand."

"WHO. THE. HELL. ARE. YOU?" She replied.

157

"The guy who makes you drive that piece of shit truck."

"Common knowledge. Anyone would know that. This is bullshit. I don't know any Pat either. GO AWAY." I was praying she would not block me. That would prevent her from even seeing any of these messages. I needed to prove to her quickly it was me.

"Someone who loves your Dracula hairline." This made her pause, so I persisted. *"Pat. Remember? The BBQ? My Commanding Officer. Last June?"* No Response. But this would make her think.

His real name was Chuck but, on that day, we razzed him and called him 'Pat' because of the way he threw the bean bags in the game of cornhole. He was a huge muscular guy who threw a bean bag like an eleven-year-old girl. So, Postman gave him the nickname 'Pat' as a joke teasing him that the name fit for either a boy or girl.

"What is today?" I sent another message.

"Thursday." She responded immediately. She remembered the BBQ. She was starting to believe.

"Ham night." I replied. Then, I followed up with: *"It's me. The Jack-ass O'Lantern carver."*

"What was the name of my dog when I was a girl?" She responded quickly. This was good. She was testing me. I was convincing her. She just needed confirmation.

"You never had a dog. You had a cat. Opus, bald behind his right ear where he picked a fight with a Blue Jay and lost. Opus was kind of an idiot. He died after choking on an odor eater." I responded.

After eleven full countdowns, she replied with only, *"David?"*

"Hi honey. Be careful with the names on an open line."

"OMG! How can this be? They told me you were killed in action. Can I call you?!?"

"Not killed. Captured. Can't talk. Only text. Hiding phone. Still captive."

"Where are you?"

"Don't know. Some desert."

"How do we get you?"

"My CO will know. You really called him, right?"

"Of course. I thought you were some stupid kid that I wanted in jail for such a mean joke."

"Not a joke."

"I know that now. OH MY GOD!"

"Wait, I have to tell you something."

"What?" She responded.

I paused. There was no dancing around this. I just needed to make it clear to her what she was facing. *"When I was captured. They tortured me."*

"What do you mean?"

"They cut me. They burned me. I don't look the same. I...have wounds. Bad ones."

"DO YOU THINK I CARE HOW YOU LOOK? I DON'T CARE! JUST COME HOME! I WANT YOU BACK! OMG! I MISS YOU! I LOVE YOU! I NEED YOU! I NEED TO CALL CHUCK BACK AND TELL HIM."

The deciphered letters were the most beautiful things I had ever seen. No music, art, or poetry had ever lifted my spirits the way these barren letters beneath shattered glass did. Something inside me soared. A light suddenly illuminated the harsh darkness. I could not help but to smile. I now knew what it must feel like to win the lottery or receive a successful transplant. For I was rich, richer than I ever dreamed, in ways I could not have even dared to imagine. My eye watered and my heart pounded. I felt like a dark shroud had been pulled from me, like an enormous weight was lifted. My breaths came in stuttering gasps and deteriorated quickly to deep-reaching sobs. My whole body wretched and twitched uncontrollably as I cried, for the first time ever—from pure, unbridled joy. And it was so much, it was overwhelming. After several long minutes of hiding out of sight, next to my dirty latrine in tears, I regained my composure and responded to the love of my life. A person that just might find a way to still love this twisted, broken man.

"No names on the line please. You don't know these people. We can't give them any information. It could be very damaging. But call Pat and tell him everything."

"He is texting me right now."

"Tell him there is a parking garage attached to this hospital. Fourth floor. It is secured, the only way out is the roof. He will know what to do. I will be there in forty-eight hours. I have to go now. I love you. I will see you soon." I powered off the phone.

Our handler Sandy told us when dealing with the government, it was unwise to allow them to dictate the schedule. "It will become a future date lost in a scheduled void." Instead, give them a date and make it tight. They will work hard and deliver. It was evil, but I had seen her do it, and it always worked. There would be no deep preparation, no full planning for my rescue. They would use the basic night op, grab and go. They would chopper in over the garage with two teams. Clear the top and work downward, level by level until they hit the bottom and controlled the entire structure. Truth was, they would not have to. I will be waiting. I will be on the top of that garage. I will be boarding the chopper before they finish securing the roof. Grab and go.

I had to prepare.

It was time for my greatest and final escape.

It was time to go home.

14. SHIT'S CREEK

Click-cluk, click-cluk. Gruel flipped the lighter open and shut as he rounded the corner. He headed slowly down the barren hall. It was late, dark, and quiet. His eyes scanned the deep heavy shadows of the corridors for anyone else. But there was no one. No surprise. Not tonight. Everyone hated this floor and avoided it like it was haunted anyway. It had no domain over Gruel though. He opened and closed his lighter some more. The echoing, *click-cluk* faded off down the long hall, disappearing into the night along with the rhythmic steps of his shoes. Then, something caught his eye. Something not right. He stared for a moment like his heart skipped a beat. He glanced around for anyone to call out to. He squinted and crinkled his forehead in confusion. He wasn't clear about what he was looking at, but one thing he was sure of, something was not right. And when something here was not right, something was very wrong. He keyed the microphone on his walkie.

"Two-seven to central." His voice was suddenly stiff. The smell and cold chill hit him at the same time. The sensation formed a new flavor of terror he had never known before today.

"Two-seven! Anyone there?" He stopped walking. Frozen, with eyes wide, he began to breathe harder. "Two-seven. Damn it, answer!"

"What do you want? We're trying to celebrate New Year's Eve. You could be here too, but you had to mouth off to the CO."

"Shut up and listen! Possible code six. I need backup." Gruel's voice was fast and tense.

"What? Are you serious or are you fucking with us? Because if I come all the way up there, someone is going to get an ass kicking. I don't care if it's you or him."

"NOW!" Gruel barked into the mic.

"Copy." The voice on the other end was far less jovial now.

Gruel released the radio and drew the gun from the holster on his belt. With the opposite hand he checked the small inconspicuous pouch on the other side of the belt. He released the snap on the flap and felt the knife inside. It was out of uniform and not permitted. His superiors had him remove it every time they noticed it, but tonight was the night he knew would come. He wanted that knife for backup. In close quarters, a knife could be even more deadly than a gun in the right hands.

Gruel retreated back to the security station never taking his eyes from the glass door of cell 715. He reached blindly over the desk and fingered clumsily at the switches. From memory and without looking, he found the light switch labeled 715 and flipped it on.

He approached the ballistic glass door and looked closer. There was no question now. He thought he could smell it from down the hall, but from here it was unmistakable and turned his stomach. A disgusting layer of shit had been smeared all over the inside of the ballistic glass door, blocking the view inside. Water poured from under the door and ran in streams down the corridors.

"What the fuck is wrong with this guy?" Gruel said aloud seemingly without meaning to. The gun trembled in his hand as the water engulfed his shoes. "Come on guys," he said, quickly glancing down the long empty hallways, hoping to see his backup. The water ran faster, the streams now forming puddles and pooling in the low parts of the floor. A thunderous *BANG!* from within the cell rattled the shit smeared door and shook the floor.

"What the fuck?" Gruel jumped back.

"HELP ME!" A desperate cry came from behind the glass entryway to cell 715. "AGGGHHHH!" *BANG!*

"What is going on in there, Captain!?" Gruel shouted. No reply. Suddenly it was deathly silent. Only the sounds of water pouring from under the door and Gruel's heavy breathing could be heard.

"Captain?" He called. No reply. "CAPTAIN!" He shouted. Silence. "Shit" He cursed. He knew the Captain was on suicide watch. He knew he might be in there dying right now. He also knew it might be a trap. But if the Captain died on his watch…after he had already fucked up…there was no telling the depths of hell he would face.

"SHIT! SHIT! SHIT! SHIT! SHIT!" Gruel cursed as he drew the keys from his belt, but hesitated to use them. He moved around the door, gripping the handle of his pistol, trying to find an angle, through the smeared shit, that would allow him a peek into the cell. Nothing. He rapped the door with his gun. "CAPTAIN!" Nothing. Louder, he banged the handle of the gun on the door. Still, no response.

"Come on, assholes!" Gruel muttered glancing down both hallways. He looked at the door and his face crinkled. Slowly, reluctantly, he moved his ear to the door, the expression on his face growing more and more disgusted. The smell made him gag and the cool glass, although clean on this side, caused him to wretch when it touched his ear. After gathering himself, Gruel tried again, this time pressing his ear to the door without gagging. Beyond the door he could hear the mixed sounds of a low moan and…gurgling.

'He's going to fucking drown," Gruel said pulling back. He held the key in front of the door lock. "SHIT! SHIT! SHIT!" He looked down the halls. Then, he glanced at his gun and at the knife in the opened pouch on his belt. Inside the Captain was unconscious, injured and drowning. If he died…. "SHIT!" Gruel shouted as he plunged the key into the lock and twisted.

It was time.

I took my place.

He kicked the door open forcefully, but it fought him and only swung slowly a little less than halfway. Water poured from around the door and splashed midway up his legs. In waves it flooded out into the hall and spread in all directions. Gruel looked down at his shoes, submerged by the water as the cool liquid penetrated through his socks to his feet. He pushed the door all the way open and peered into the dark room with his gun pointed out in front of him. Gruel drew his flashlight from his belt and clicked it on. Something was very wrong. The light in the cell should be on.

"Captain?" He called out. "What did you do to the light? Where are you?" He moved slowly into the cell clearing the short bathroom wall. As he rounded, he heard the gurgling again, but it was not coming from the floor. It was coming from high up, like near the ceiling.

Gruel looked up and caught sight of me standing on top of my toilet seat. I spit the water in my mouth at him and held my hands carefully behind my back.

"WHA—!?" Gruel jumped back in a splash. "HANDS! HANDS UP OR I SHOOT! DON'T MOVE!" His eyes where large and filled with terror. He glanced back at the door repeatedly. His nose was wrinkled from the stench and his hands shook worse than mine, forcing the barrel of his gun to dance all over. He glanced down beneath my feet to the toilet clogged with mattress stuffing. Water poured out as it overflowed endless gallons from over the bowl, but under the dry plastic seat I was standing upon.

"What size are you?" I asked.

"PUT YOUR FUCKING HANDS UP!" He demanded, shouting loud enough that they could hear him in the next year.

I grinned slowly moving my hands out from behind my back exposing the contents of my left grip. It did not occur to him right away what I was holding. He blinked stupidly at it several times, then his eyes followed it up into the ceiling where the wire emerged. It had been attached to the room's only light fixture. The fixture had been dismantled and it left a large hole in the sheetrock ceiling. His eyes again traced the long white wire emerging from the hole, down to my hand, then to the very end where the exposed copper wires glistened off the beam of his flashlight. It took me hours to pull every inch of slack in the wire to get it long enough to just reach. I suspect, for a moment, he thought I was trying to hang myself. Then he glanced down at the water, up to my feet standing on the dry toilet seat and then, one more time up to the light fixture the wire had been powering.

Finally, it hit him.

"What the…. Oh, F—" He never finished the profanity. I dropped the wire onto the flooded floor of the cell and Gruel began to jerk and dance. Teeth gritted, eyes clenched shut, he went completely stiff and shook rapidly like he was having a seizure. Concrete exploded from the wall behind me as his gun accidentally discharged. The bulb in the flashlight he held grew ultra-bright and then popped, throwing the cell back into darkness. I watched him twitch for a few long moments and just when he was looking like he was going to fall over, I pulled the wire from the water. He groaned and dropped to his knees with a splash, whisps of smoke curling from his hair. He gasped for breath and vomited into the swirling water. The gray patch of beard under his lower lip was no longer gray.

"What size are you?"

Four men ran down the hall splashing with each step while sharing their confusion and indignation at the flood. I was slightly disappointed that other than Gruel, there were only four guards in sector seven tonight. It seems my intimidation was wearing off. Perhaps I was not the threat I thought I was?

"What the hell!? Where is all this water coming from?" One guard asked no one in particular.

"Shut up and focus!" Another larger soldier replied and drew his weapon as they slowed and approached the slightly opened cell door.

"OH CHRIST!" The first guard gasped. "It is! It's a fucking code six! He's out! He's fucking out!"

"SHUT THE FUCK UP!"

They looked at the door. The water poured from under and around it, feeding the flooded floor. From inside the cell, they could hear a muffled cry. The largest guard pushed on the door. It did not move.

"He's not out! He is still in there!"

"Is that what I think it is on the door?"

"*Ohhhhfff.* That's the smell!"

"What's with the water!?"

"SHUT UP!" The largest of the guards commanded the other three. He keyed his walkie and spoke into it "One-five to two-seven. What's your twenty?" The muffled cries behind the door grew in volume and intensity at the sound of his voice. From the radio came no response. "Two-seven, come in." The four men stood waiting and looking around anxiously. "Where is he?" the guard asked no one in particular. "Two-seven?"

"We are going to have to open this door." Another guard said. They all looked at each other knowing he was right.

"I'd rather lick that door than open it," one mumbled.

"Fuuuuuck!" Said another. They looked around nervously as the large guard took control. He keyed his mic again.

"One-five to central." He hesitated as if the words hurt him to say. "Code six. Better get the Doc up here. It's time to get ready." He released the mic and turned to his men.

"Alright, you and you are on me." He turned to the smallest of them and said "You stay back and watch our backs. Stay in the hall and watch the door." The small guard nodded nervously.

"Omar, you got this?"

"Yea…Yes! Yes!" He tried to sound ready.

"Don't let anyone come up behind us. Do you understand? Can you do this?"

"Yes…yes, sir!" Jesus, I could almost hear the young soldier's teeth chattering in fear.

"Weapons ready. Try not to shoot him, this is live ammo. The tranqs won't arrive until Doc does. We need to try to control him until then. If we are facing a mortal situation, defend yourself. Fire if you have to. Let's go." The lead guard commanded. That is when I noticed the bandages on his right bicep. Hey, I know this guy. He was the square jawed soldier. It was good to see him again.

This was going to be perfect.

I just needed the timing to work out.

The square jawed guard placed a hand on the door. With two soldiers flanking just off his shoulders, each with a gun at the ready, he pushed the door open sending a wave of water through the cell and hallway. The light in the room was unsteady and blinked in uneven flashes of dim illumination. The three men entered the cell as one. The last soldier stood outside looking nervously down each hall.

He would crack.

Soon.

The square jawed soldier, deepest in the cell, saw the silhouette at once. It was illuminated by an out-of-place, flickering orange glow. His gun was on the man. He halted the group as he fumbled his flashlight. The man screamed a muffled scream over and over, louder and louder. The flashlight beam cut the room and flashed streaks upon the far wall as he recovered his grip and control. As the square jawed soldier's flashlight steadied, it lit Gruel's face, and the hair on the back of his neck stood full upright. The sight was chilling.

Stripped down to only boxer shorts, Gruel was tied up with what looked like torn strips of a mattress. He was gagged with a mouth full of mattress stuffing. He was arched back, hog-tied in reverse, with his hands and feet behind him. He was on his knees, bent backwards with a line that bound around his feet and stretched tightly up across his eyes, arching him painfully backward to the point he could not move.

"What the fuck!?" The lead guard said as they all grabbed at the bindings in attempt to free their distressed colleague. With every pull of the fabric strips the muffled screams grew in volume and intensity. Finally, one guard pulled the stuffing from Gruel's mouth.

"GET OUT! GET OUT!" He shouted instantly! "IT'S A TRAP! THE POWER LINE! THE LIGHTER!"

At that very same moment, one of the guards also shouted, "Oh, shiiiiiiit!" The square jawed soldier spun around. He looked past Gruel and noticed the source of the flickering orange illumination in the room.

Hanging from a hole in the ceiling was a wire, raw and sparking. It was being held up, just above the overflowing water by a single, thin fabric strip tied to the destroyed light fixture in the ceiling hole above. The Zippo lighter was tied into the center of the strip, halfway up. The Zippo was open, lit and slowly burning the fabric in two.

When the guard outside the door, heard the shouting and mention of a trap, he knew he had to help his team. He was new and could show them, right now, that he was worthy of their respect. He rotated and pointed his gun into the cell taking a step forward. He took in the scene and his eyes went wide.

Before the splashing sounds behind him registered, my foot hit him square in the back, sending him crashing with an enormous splash into the cell. I slammed the cell door shut and cranked the key, locking it. Then, I bent the key sharply to one side, then the other, breaking it off in the lock. I had less than seconds. I sprinted as fast as anyone can in ankle-deep water, lunging onto the top of the huge wooden security station desk.

Then time ran out.

Before any of them could grab it, the lighter burned through the fabric strip. As it came apart, the wire fell down into the water. From atop the desk, I could hear the screams and electrical popping. The lights in the hall flickered and dimmed. Even around the huge wooden security desk, I could hear the electricity snapping and cracking at the wires and metal pieces submerged in the ankle-deep water. I let it go on for several seconds while I searched the desk for the light switch labeled 715. I flipped the switch and the shouting and popping stopped. The lights of the hallways stabilized. I heard several splashes from the cell as they toppled to the floor. Moans filled the room and leaked out into the hallway.

Just for shits and giggles, I flipped the switch on again and after a few seconds, back off. A whimper joined the moans. I jumped off the counter and started to move. I grabbed the mic on my new uniform that Gruel reluctantly agreed to loan me.

"Two-seven to central. Code six, need backup!" I barked in a voice of desperation. I looked around the security station. Not a single hat. I wondered briefly if they were banned.

"Central to two-seven." My walkie crackled. "Sit rep, please advise." They were asking for a situation report and recommendation. Interesting. Someone had been feeding them our communications procedures and they were using them.

"Two-seven to central." I began, "Sector six, send everyone you have!" I barked trying to sound desperate and terrified.

"Copy, two-seven."

Copy? What the hell did that mean? Were they sending them all?

Well, shit.

I was not expecting that. I expected some push back and then finally, I thought they might send a few. I totally oversold it. But I needed this to happen. Yes, you heard me right. I *needed* to see where they are coming from. You see, I don't know exactly where sector six is. It is not spelled out on the blueprints and I don't have time to just roam around and find it. So, a bunch of armed dudes are going to emerge from some door in just a moment. That door will be the door to sector six. That door will be the one I need to go through. All I have to do is wait. They will show me the way.

I looked over my shoulder to the thick steel door behind the security desk. That was it. My way out. No steel barred levels of security, no skiff, no chipped tile. According to the blueprints in my pocket, on the other side of that door was a security tunnel that led to the parking garage. I am sure it is secure and difficult to pass, but it was a straight shot and I have not come across a security barrier I have not gotten through at least once. This would be no different. If Chuck shows up with a chopper ride home on the other side of this door, I would only ever need to clear it once. I patted the door like it was a big dog.

"I'll be back for you," I said.

I looked down each of the long hallways. I knew what I needed to do. There were three entrances/exits to this sector. I will pick a door that I think leads to sector six and hide behind it. I have a one in three chance to get it right. When they come rushing in, I will slide right out behind them, and into sector six before they even know what is going on.

I picked a door and flattened up against the wall behind where it would swing open. Any moment n…

Just then, the door all the way at the opposite end of this long hall slammed open.

Shit. Wrong door.

And I was out in the open, in plain sight.

I pulled the mic from my walkie off my shoulder and held it up high in front of my face to hide the hideousness and reduce the chance of them recognizing me instantly. "Seven one five!" I shouted and pointed to the shit-smeared door. They splashed their way down the hall looking baffled and confused. Luckily, they were too confused and preoccupied by the smell of shit, burning hair and electrical wires, as well as the ankle-deep flood to pay much attention to me. I rushed over to the security booth and darted behind the desk. I was barking orders the whole time.

"Stack up on that door!" and "Hurry, he is going to breach! Move!!"

As they approached the door, not more than twenty feet away, the front soldier called out to me.

"What the hell is that smell!?"

I lowered the mic and grinned that crooked half-working face grin and replied,

"That is the smell of Shit's Creek! Hope you brought a paddle."

The faces of all five of them went white as I flicked the main light switch off. The hall went pitch black as I jumped up on the desk with my finger still on the light switch for cell 715. I heard them finally moving, splashing toward me.

I flipped the switch.

I could not see any of them, but the soldier closest to me made a "*GA-GA-GA-GA-GA-GA!*" shuttering sound while the screams and wails of the other men filled the corridor and cell 715. I flicked the hall lights on for just a second to take in each of their positions as they jerked and twitched in place under the jolting of electricity. I studied my path. Then, I snapped all the light switches off at once.

I ran in the darkness for the door they entered through. Each of them collapsed into the toilet water flood in moans and grunts of pain. None of them rose back up as I waved Gruel's key card at the card reader. The reader beeped, flashed green and clicked open.

"Happy new year!" I shouted.

Then, I left sector seven a free man.

A free man—with a strut.

15. OVER THE PAINBOW

177

I walked with purpose, but not so much that I appeared hurried. My uniform was wet. My shoes squeaked on the floor as I walked. The weight of the gun was pulling the belt down. So, I shifted and tightened it as I walked.

I wish I had a hat and sunglasses. My face was a real problem. Grotesquely unique, it posed the greatest risk for ruining this whole escape. It could screw everything up. But so far, things were going my way. I guess it was just dumb luck that today turned out to be minimally staffed.

Then suddenly, I stopped. Before me was the door I was looking for. I glanced at it and then down the long hall to ensure I was alone. Whoa. Things really *were* going my way for a change.

The number next to the door read 612.

Holy shit.

I could see the light beneath the door and could hear someone moving around inside. I reached out and touched the door. It was an old steel door with the sliding medal shutter like I used to have on my cell. But there was no lock, no place to put a key in.

Slowly, I slid the shutter open quietly. There, in the cell, was Postman. He was dressing hurriedly.

"Sir, I need you to sign for this package," I said in a low quiet voice. He spun with wide eyes. He looked shocked at first, then giggled that high and intoxicating laugh.

"God damn!" he said as if I scared him. "Captain!? How in almighty hell did you get out again!?" He smiled. "What in hell did you do?"

"Later. Time to go. They are right behind me," I said, searching the door. "How does this open?" I asked pulling on the handle.

"There is a switch at the security booth." He pointed to the large desk peeking out around the corner. This was set up similar to sector seven.

"No key?"

"No. Just the switch," he replied.

"How many guards at the booth?"

"Today? At this time of night? Maybe one. I just saw a bunch of them haul'n ass that way." Postman motioned at the door I had entered through. "That was probably for you, huh?" I pressed flat up against the wall and slid down towards the huge wooden desk.

I approached the corner and peeked around. Damn. No one there. This was almost easy. From behind the desk, I quickly searched the grid of switches. 612. There it was. I poked it. Back in the direction of Postman, I heard the door lock release with a loud *KA-CLUNK*. I looked down both halls. No one. We were still good. Postman rounded the corner pointing back at the door I just came through.

"Come on! I know the way to the garage!"

"No. This way." I pointed in another direction. I pulled the blueprint out and unfolded it. "It should be that door, right there," I said looking over the large page that was still half-folded. "Yep. Here." I jabbed a finger at the paper, looked up at the door just to the right of the security booth. It was marked with a sign that I think read "Stairs."

"Come on, we have to go. Now!" I folded the map and headed for the door. Postman hesitated for a moment, looking back in the direction of his cell.

"You want a moment to say goodbye to your cell?" I asked with a chuckle as I swiped Gruel's ID card at the reader and pushed the stairway door open as it blinked green.

"But this way is the..." he began.

"We need to do something first. We'll double back. Let's go, they will be here any second!" Postman hesitated, then fell in behind me.

We rounded down the stairs at a full run. Each floor I paused to peer out the small window in the exit doors until I found what I was looking for. I opened the door slowly. Honest to god, I said a prayer as we darted to the large double doors only about six feet away. Postman slid up behind me as I swiped the ID at the card reader and it turned green.

I almost giggled.

Suddenly the alarm sounded, ringing out and filling the night with the sounds of that damn siren. Red bulbs mounted high on the walls illuminated and cast a red haze over everything.

I flung the door open and pulled Postman inside. As I closed the heavy doors quickly behind us, the locks clicked into place. I looked around the power room. It was about a ten by fifteen foot, poorly-lit room, cast in the same red tint from the alarm. The ceiling and walls were lined with pipes, wires, and conduits. On the opposite wall was a bank of electrical panels. In the center of the wall was my target. A very large panel, more than three times the size of the others. In the corner, beside the door, leaned various tools. I grabbed a pair of coveralls off the hook and handed them to Postman.

"Put these on." I grabbed a shovel and moved over to the lock on the large panel. Finding the best angle, I held the shovel over my head like a spear.

"What are we doing?" Postman asked as he pulled on the coveralls.

I stabbed the shovel at the lock. With a loud *CRACK!* it broke into pieces that skipped and spun across the dark floor. I grabbed the large panel gate and swung it open. It was the size of a closet door. The breakers inside hummed and smelled of ozone.

"It's time to go." I moved into a fierce stance, holding the shovel like I was going to hit a home run. "Get ready, I'm not really sure what this will do."

He looked at the shovel. He looked at the panel.

"No," he said just above a whisper. "Don't do this." He reached out for the shovel. "You don't know what you are doing."

"I do," I said. "And it looks like you know what I am doing too." I grinned with the half of my mouth that still moved. "And it will work."

"It will." He replied back quickly. His voice sounded stressed. "I'm sure of it. But don't you realize what that will do?" I paused and lowered the shovel a little bit. What the hell was he talking about?

"Of course I realize what it will do. I kill the power to the building. There will be sheer chaos. Security will be overwhelmed. In our snazzy little uniforms, we will blend in, easily making our way back up to the fourth floor where we will take the hall to the garage. Then we rendezvous with Chuck and take the road out of hell."

"We don't have to kill the building's grid," he said.

"Postman, what the fuck are you talking about? The power is the key! That is the problem that is bigger than us! Security won't be able to focus on us if the grid is down! *This* is how we escape. *This* is the piece I have been missing!"

"This won't just kill the power... It will short the system. Even the backup generator will fail... The cell doors are electronically sealed. They will be open. It is a faulty system being replaced with something more secure. Right now, if you kill that grid, only one door in this building will remain locked." Something in his voice made me pause. I looked into his eyes. There was fear there. Concern.

"The shiny new glass door of 715, right?" I asked.

"Right...I can't let you do this." He shook his head and his voice changed. That slight southern drawl was gone. It was quiet and reserved now. In one quick motion he snatched the shovel from my hand.

"What the fuck, Postman!?"

"All those people. No. This was a mistake. You were supposed to take the hall to the garage. Not this. They were right."

"Postman?"

His eyes were staring off in the distance. Deep in a scenario he was unfolding in his own head and trying to find a way out.

I punched him.

Hard.

"Come to your damn senses!" My voice was gravelly with anger.

"WAIT! YOU WILL ENDANGER THE LIVES…OF EVERYONE IN THIS HOSPITAL!" He wiped the blood from his mouth, trying to speak while it garbled his words. "I can't let you…" he spat blood onto the floor "…do this."

"What the fuck is wrong with you!?" I barked.

"Listen to me!" He begged. "Damn it!" He cursed angrily, his head down, his fists balled. It occurred to me; his curse was not aimed at me. He seemed to be directing it to himself. "You are in a hospital. A mental hospital," he said. "The D.R. Ross Mental Facility."

"So? We knew that. That is the best way to make a medicinal prison work." My voice was angry and my words twisted. Then my brain engaged, registering his words and starting to piece it together.

"Wait…" I paused "What did you say? Do you mean…did you just say…"

"I don't know what you did for him. I tried to find out, but it's all classified. Anyway, he feels like he owes you."

"Wait…what are you talking about?"

"Steve McMillian," he said.

"Steve…" My voice whispered. My mind raced. More and more. Things started falling into place. Faint images, conversations. It began to come together. Pictures formed. Feelings mounted and connected. "I remember…Senator McMillian," I heard myself say. "Yes. It was for him. He was why we were there…."

"Where?" Postman asked quickly.

"Pakistan. Yes, we were hunting. That damn Cuban guy. The operative. We were not even to alpha point." I was lost in the memories. Swimming in a churning ocean of disjointed recollections, all raging to find their place. I was talking through them; I was trying to piece them together. "The Humvee was hit. It was fast. Professional. We never saw it coming."

"Where were you before that?"

"Before…I don't… WAIT! On leave. I had just flown home. To the family. That fucking piece of shit truck would not start. It broke down in the airport parking lot… She was so pissed…"

"What was her name?"

"Kelly. Oh god how I miss her. Just looking at her…. She was the reason I did any of it. To keep her safe. Keep them safe. My family… On that day I…" It was all coming together. I could almost see it all.

"Where did you fly in from?"

"Iraq. I fucking hate that pla—" Suddenly a red flag went up in my head. My eyes shot back into focus. I glared at him. I know this line of questioning. It couldn't be. Am I that stupid? My hand shot forward and snatched at the nappy and matted hair on his head.

The wig came off.

The makeup covering his face stopped just short of his hairline creating a strange lighter toned frame around his face. It was not Postman. It was never Postman. Never. In the crates? Nope. It was this bastard. He played me for a fool. His wide eyes stared back at me unknowing how to handle the situation.

"Fuck you, Brian!" I hissed. He opened his mouth to respond.

"I'm not—"

I punched him.

Harder this time. As hard as I could. I meant to do damage.

Another rage-filled right cross caught his nose at a slight angle. The impact did not drive straight back, but just to the side, enough for the cartilage to take the brunt of the blow. And it did. His nose snapped and I landed another just before the blood began to pour from his nostrils.

The shovel clattered to the floor. Brian staggered and doubled over to drain the blood when I stepped forward and drilled his bent-over form with a knee to the face. The force took his feet out from beneath him and he landed flat on his back with the sound of meat hitting concrete.

I jumped on top of him and began hammering. There was no technique here, just a wrath of punches intending to inflict as much pain as I was in right now. Punch after punch, blow after blow. Each one as hard as I could swing. My knuckles crunched and cracked, the skin swelling quickly and splitting from the force of impact. I could not feel it at all. For there was no more pain to feel. I had reached my limit and if not rage blinded, I would have been surprised that emotional pain could eclipse physical pain in such a way.

Then my elbow went tight. It pulled in quick and sharply lunged my shoulder forward. Brian rolled me. Suddenly I found myself beneath him. He was mounted on my chest and fought to pin me flat on my back. I quickly shrimped my hips to the side and tipped us both on an angle. His leg shot out wide to stabilize his position, but it was too late. I slid my hand under his leg and pushed it up and over, to throw him off me. But suddenly it went loose. The leg slid up over my shoulder and wrapped around my neck.

Shit.

He was setting up a triangle. A leg choke around my neck that would render me unconscious in seconds. I pulled my other elbow in before he could trap the arm and then I slid it through his legs quickly to give me an escape out the back. We wrestled for position and I found myself suddenly on his back. I went for the choke to put Brian to sleep, but before I could lock it in, he pushed my arm up and sunk his teeth into my forearm.

Fucker.

When I did not immediately release the choke, he repositioned and took a bigger bite. This time I let go and kicked him away. We staggered onto our feet. *Jujitsu* was fantastic but you had to be close for it to work. Those opponents not fighting for points, but instead fighting for their lives often fought beyond the rules. Beyond honor. When you had an opponent that was willing to bite, stab, eye gouge, punch you in the neck or groin, and so on, it was time to switch to another fighting system that gained some distance away from them.

He rubbed at his eyes and then lunged forward with a quick kick that did not include power from his hips. I knew right away it was a feint. I just tapped it away and put my hands up, covering my head, where I knew the real attack was coming. Sure enough, here came the big punch to the face. In a fraction of a second, I deflected the punch and entered into his momentum.

This technique ends fights instantly. It is called *iriminage*. To those outside Bushikan Aikido, it looked a

186

little like a "clothesline" move you would see on old T.V. wrestling. One wrestler would get his opponent bouncing off the ropes then charge at him with one arm out. That arm would hit his opponent in the neck knocking him down, comically at times. Ours was not comical. Ours created a circle from torque fueled by the punch. It was short, quick, and explosive. When done properly it took opponents clean off their feet at almost neck level, dropping them hard on the ground, with their head taking all of the impact. It was a deadly technique that took years to master and just as long to learn to be able to receive the technique without getting seriously hurt.

In a blur, my arm crossed over in front of his neck as my other hand slammed his hips forward, forcing him into the technique. I cut down sharp and strong.

Oh, I had him.

I felt his head snap back and his feet come off the ground. I eagerly waited for the head to drop down and crash onto the concrete floor.

This fight was over.

But something strange happened. He went almost weightless. I felt a hand wrap around my upper arm and heard the slap of his other open hand on concrete to break his fall. Brian landed on the floor almost gently, rolled backward, and popped back up. His face smeared with blood from his nose and bad makeup, his eyes were squinty and watering profusely. He swung blindly and wildly.

I deflected the looping punch to cross him up again. Moving in, I jammed my shoulder under his elbow. I ducked my head, rotated my hips, and pulled his wrist down into a *shihonage* that would break his arm.

Brian went weightless again as he again performed a full breakfall. He moved rapidly with the torque, rolling over my shoulder, flipping through the air, slapping the concrete with his other arm. He once again, absorbed the technique and impact of the fall. When I spoke earlier about the years of training needed to be able to receive the techniques without getting injured, it is called *ukemi*. It is the art of falling. It is a hard-earned, painful skill that many failed to ever master. It saved you from these brutal techniques at full speed. This was it. And Brian had mastered it.

But *how*?

Bushikan Aikido was a different form of the art. My own form. Our techniques were unique and so was our *ukemi*. There was maybe a handful of people on the planet that ever mastered it. And I personally taught every one of them. So how did this shitbag know it?

Brian slowly pulled himself to his feet. Then lunged forward blindly swinging. A streak of silver arced towards me. I ducked just a second before the shovel sliced the air. I'm not sure it would have hit me anyway. Brian took a solid stance. He held the shovel out in front of him like he was holding a *jo* staff. Clever. His eyes were still watering and barely open. He was fighting to keep the nose blood from pouring into his mouth or down the back of his throat.

"HELP! IN HEEEEERE! HEEEEELP!!" he screamed, his eyes blinking wildly.

Crazy how that happens. The nerve ending from your nose affects your eyes. It doesn't happen to everyone, but it happens to me too. Well, it happened the first time I got my nose broken, anyway.

"IN HEEEEEEEERE!" he shouted again, shaking his head side to side like he could break free from the effects of the broken nose and regain clear vision.

"What did you do to Postman?" I demanded. Brian squinted, corrected his stance to face me, then blinked again and lunged forward with the shovel. I stepped aside, released the retention strap on the holster and drew the gun from my belt.

Brian froze. He might not have been able to see it, but he heard it.

In that instant, I kicked hard at the side of his knee. The impact was tremendous. The sound was disgusting. His knee bent at a strange, incorrect angle and then folded like a lawn chair.

A broken lawn chair.

He collapsed to the ground in a heap with a cry of pain.

"I have waited for this, you bastard," I said calmly. Then I racked the slide on the gun.

Brian, sat up straight like a drunk suddenly sobering up. His ears perked up and turned to face me.

"Wait!" He shifted into a crawl, wincing with each movement. "WAIT!" he shouted. All composure lost. All his calm demeanor thrown aside. "You don't want to do this! You don't want to do this!" His voice cracked. His tone pleading. He stumbled forward blindly over the shovel. His right hand, tangled in the handle. He fell forward slamming his face and nose off the floor. He cried out on impact as a new wave of blood poured forth from his nose and mouth.

I took aim. I steadied my breath and found the bead. It was never real. I thought this was a friend. I listened to him. The things he convinced me to do. The things he made me consider. Every word was from this prick was a lie. None of it was from the man I thought I trusted and knew. It was all wrong. All of my current plans were based on our conversation. He had set me up from the beginning. It was time to change course. Now that I knew, things seemed clear. I knew what I had to do.

I lowered the gun, pausing for a moment. It was so obvious now; what I needed to do. I holstered the weapon and reached for the phone in my back pocket. I powered it on while Brian staggered around on the floor blubbering and spitting blood everywhere. Six percent. Plenty of charge. This would only take a minute. I punched in 1221 to unlock the phone, then opened the messenger. I poked the conversation with the Ball and Chain image.

"Always remember I love you." I dictated quietly. "If you ever really knew how much, it would scare you." I took a deep breath and swallowed hard. "It is time to move on." My eyes welled up and I fought back the emotion of everything this meant.

"It will be alright." I ended it.

Then I pressed the Send button.

Quickly, I powered off the phone to prevent receiving a reply. I know what I have to do. I tossed the phone on the ground. If possible, shattering the screen more.

It was time.

"This is it. This is my moment of clarity." My voice was dry and raspy. "You talked so much about it. Here it is. I am going to kill you. And then they will kill me." I tried to smile, but I did not have it in me. I had liked my life. I had loved it. I had loved those in it. Until this monster took it all away from me. Now, I wanted nothing more than to end it all. Now, I knew how.

"I am a coward no more."

"Wait!" Brian cried out. As I stepped closer, he raised his arms over his head in a defensive position, still trying to clear his vision. I grabbed his fingers in the same *yubi dori* technique he used to break my thumb. I torqued until I heard the snap and crunch of bone. Brian moaned in pain collapsing back to the ground, blindly entangled in the shovel once more.

"That is for my wife and son!" I growled stepping back and raising the gun. "And Postman!" I cocked back the gun's hammer. "And my whole damn team!"

"Wait! This was not the moment of clarity I was talking about. You have it all wrong! So close! No! Please, no!" He shifted onto all fours, then looked up at me. Raising a hand, his mangled fingers skewed in strange grotesque angles. I could not tell if he was reaching for me or holding up a hand in a 'stop' gesture. "There is so much you need to—"

In a brilliant one-legged launch, Brian shot upward and forward, the shovel out in front of him, cutting the air in a blur. I had been baiting him, hoping for him to do something like this. I was ready. I moved aside, exposing the open electrical panel I was standing in front of. As his attack passed by, I pushed him hard on the back adding to his momentum. The shovel just missed my gun as it streaked through the air. Brian lost all footing from the extra force I added to his lunge. Instinctively, he tried to recover but as soon as he put weight on his injured knee, he stumbled and spilled forward.

191

The shovel sank deep into the electrical panel and the room lit up like the surface of the sun. Brilliant blue-white lightning arced from the box to the ceiling, then to the wall and finally to Brian who collapsed to the floor once more. Smoke and fire sprung from everywhere the lightning touched, and the shovel burst into flames as the lights flashed twice, three times, and flickered out altogether.

Brian rolled upon the floor, grunting and groaning, pounding at the flames in his beard and on his coveralls. The shovel, with its wooden handle on fire, fell from the electrical panel and clattered onto the floor in a cloud of smoke.

I watched Brian rolling and thrashing at the flames as the emergency lighting kicked in and the foul smell of burnt hair and electrical fire filled the room.

What would those flames do to his face? I thought of my own grotesque scars.

Damn it.

I ripped my shirt off and jumped on the asshole, covering his burning beard. I patted it all down until only the roll of smoke and stench emerged. I stood up and stepped back. Brian threw the shirt off his face and pulled himself upright against the wall just below the huge smoldering panel. Half his beard had been burned away exposing the left side of his face down to the skin. Instinctively, I touched the left side of my melted ice cream face. I looked at Brian and was strangely relieved to see the fire may have burned him but did not scar or deform his skin. His clothes still smoldered, he was beaten, broken, and bloody, but he was unscarred. We seemed to realize at the same time what I had just done.

"You sav…" Brian began.

"Shut up." I commanded.

Suddenly something on the floor next to him buzzed and vibrated in an arc. Instinctively he reached for it, but his pain made him freeze. A look of utter panic took over his half-bearded face. The screen was lit, a text message had arrived.

"That your phone?" I asked "Did that fall out of your pocket during our figh…" I started to ask. At once we both lunged for it. It was no fight. He could not see well, was moving like he had been run over by a truck and it was easy to pry his broken fingers off the phone. I flipped the flat black rectangular device over and over, pressing every button I could until the screen illuminated again.

And there it was.

A blue bubble in the middle of the screen displayed the received text message:

"Always remember I love you. If you ever really knew how much, it would scare…"

The blood drained from my body. My hands shook, uncontrollably jerking in spasmodic rhythms. My heart pounded so hard I could feel it in my one good ear. My breath was coming in rapid gasps.

"How did you…. Wha…? Who…? She…?" I stammered like a desperate junkie pleading with a dealer. I looked at Brian. "I…I was never really talking to her?" I whispered. It was all I could manage. "It was you…?"

"But…"

"No…"

"Please… No…" I stammered on.

193

It felt like my soul collapsed. A feeling so crushing, so intricately painful no language possessed the words to describe it. And here I thought I had already found the very deepest depths of suffering.

I was such a fool.

It could hurt so much more. So, so much. I dropped to my knees. From somewhere deep inside me, a place so old and tucked away I never knew it existed, came a shutter of sorrow that unleashed an anguish I have not experienced since before the innocence of youth. I sobbed deeper and more completely than I had ever before.

This was it.

The end.

I want out.

Stop the pain.

Stop.

The.

Pain.

Please. God. Grant me one wish. Make the pain stop or give me the courage to end it...

And suddenly, as if god answered my prayer, I had it. I sat up, mud from the tears and the dirty floor streaked my morbid face. Where was it? Where the fuck was it? My hand closed around the grip and I pulled it from the holster. Whatever was on the other side of this bullet could not be as painful as what I felt right now.

It was time to find out.

"NO!" Brian barked through his squinted eyes. "NOOOOO!" He shuffled trying to sit up higher, but he was a mess and barely able to move. I put the gun to my head. "NNNOOOOO! HELP ME! SOMEONE HEEEELP! DON'T DO IT! PLEAAAAASE!" he shouted with a horror and pain I could relate to. He shouted as he deteriorated into sobs. I paused looking at him. His sounds echoed what I was feeling. It was like the unique howl of a pack of wolves, a sound only those within the pack knew. Those sobs were familiar. Some pain in the degree of which I was going through. I looked at him. This was more than a job to him. More than just the intel.

"Wait! Don't do it! Please, please... Please!" He pleaded with me as if I had the gun pointed at him. As if it was his life on the end of this barrel. "Wait...no...you don't deserve this. This is my fault. Don't do it!" He put his hands out in front of him defensively as he looked around. Then he started patting his pockets. "Here...here..." He pulled out a pocket notebook and tore a page out. He drew on the page three circles, one inside the other.

A target.

He then positioned it over his stomach.

"Here! Point the gun here!" he pleaded with me, "Point the damned gun here!" he commanded.

Suddenly something inside me broke. Rage overtook the sorrow and the world went suddenly red. He was right. This fucker played me for a fool. It was him. All fucking him. It was never her; it was never Postman; it was always this fucker. He stole my life, my family, my future. I can fix this all right now. He was the only one I told, the only one I leaked info to. The only leak. If he never leaves this room, it never happened. He was what kept me from my family. Him. All him. For all I knew, and I strongly

195

suspected, this was Dr. Idnkel. He pulled nervously at his ear.

"Right here!" He shook the little paper. "As...ass...asshole!" He struggled with the word. It was the first curse I ever heard him hurl at me. I pulled the barrel from my head and pointed it at the paper. One shot makes so much right. I shoot him, then, they kill me.

Coward no more.

I grinded my teeth in rage. Tears streaked my face. So much pain. So deep the hurt. My chest heaved and I got a bead on the tiny paper target. One shot.

Just pull.

Something felt wrong. I looked at the paper.

"Up, asshole!" I barked. He stared at me confused. "I know what you are doing. Move it up!"

"What?" He looked confused. His eyes still watered and fluttered as he spat blood away.

"The target is too fucking low. That is your stomach. You could survive that. Over the heart! Put it over the heart!"

His hands shook and his chest started to heave as he slowly dragged the paper up and to the left. Right there. I took a bead and steadied the gun. I slowed my breathing and lined up the sights. One bullet. My hands shook and I was fighting my breath. I looked over the gun and noticed he moved the target back to his stomach.

"What the fuck? I'll fix this!" I raged, holstering the gun harshly and pulling Gruel's knife from the other side of the belt. I jumped on top of Brian, pulling the paper target from his hand and tossing it onto floor. I grabbed his shirt and ripped it open exposing his chest. Like a fucking deranged cultist, I carved the target into his chest over his heart. Not deep, just enough to make it visible. Brian did not make a sound.

I stood back up and stepped backward drawing the gun once more.

"It won't move this time," I said as I took aim.

"Wait." Brian said. His voice was back to calm. He knew what was coming and seemed to have made peace with it. "One more thing… No tricks…I promise… I will not fight you… Just one last request, soldier to soldier." Gingerly, he leaned over attempting to pick up the notepad. Wincing multiple times in pain, he finally instead pulled an old, folded up paper from a pocket beneath his coveralls. His twisted fingers scribbled something down and then he tossed the folded yellowed paper at my feet. He sat back up with a groan and spread his arms out to his sides giving me a clear view of the morbid target.

"What does it say?" I asked.

"I wrote it down because you will forget. Please keep it with you. It is my last request between soldiers. Please, please honor it. Keep it with you." His voice was calm. His eyes closed.

"WHAT DOES IT SAY!?" I demanded. The shout echoed loudly in the small smoke-filled room.

"Something that you will need to know," he said, then spat more blood onto the floor. "I forgive you," he finally responded.

I glanced down.

It did. In large block letters it read "I FORGIVE YOU."

"FUCK YOU!" I shouted.

"It is not your fault. I forgive you."

"SHUT THE FUCK UP!" I tried to squeeze the trigger, but something stopped me. He looked at me, with his watering eyes and battered bloody nose. He coughed and spat blood on the floor one last time. He closed his eyes and tipped his head back, as if he were a million miles away reliving some glorious moment. Then, for the first time ever, Brian smiled.

"It's OK. I forgive you."

"I'm going t…" I started but something lodged in my brain and the threat jarred in my throat as my eye locked onto something so unique, it could not be mistaken.

"How…" I stammered; my one eye wide. "It can't…"

It could not be. It *could not*.

There, on the red, fire kissed skin of his cheek, where his beard had been burned away, dimples highlighted the end of his smile. Two of them. Stacked like a snowman.

"Wha…. How…"

No.

Suddenly my world started coming apart as recollections triggered and began to fall into place. Memories formed; recall took over. Vast portions of my life suddenly fell into place.

No…

My whole body shook. I looked at the target shallowly carved into his chest. It was three *squares*, one inside the other, not three circles.

Well, have you ever tried to carve a round hole with a straight blade?

I suddenly looked at my left forearm, now bare from the removal of my shirt to put out the fire in Brian's beard. The emergency lighting glowed off the dirty and scarred skin. I looked at the letters and back to the square target. Then back to the dimples.

No.

I dropped the gun to my side and stared closely at my arm. I blinked dumbfoundedly as the blocky letters that made up DR IDNKEL suddenly shifted.

Round hole, straight blade.

The letters looked more like squares than capital *D*s. I had assumed they were capital *D*s. But now... What if they were not? What if they were the round *circles* that *I* carved?

For the first time I read the scars properly. For the first time I read the squares as circles. As *O*s not *D*s.

"ORIONKEL"

"ORION KEL"

"Orion..."

"...Kel..."

No...

"We stopped you before you could finish her name," Brian said from the floor. "Go on. You know what it was supposed to say. You said it earlier, but I don't think you caught it with everything that was happening. Go on. Read it. You know what it says now. You remember her name now."

"Orion…" My voice croaked in pain. "…Kelly…" I whispered, the tears streaming from my eyes like the blood from Brian's nose. "I remember their names…I just wanted to remember their names. I did this…" I fought back the tears. "I carved this into my arm to remember their names…"

"That's right." Brian's own voice shuttered.

Wait, not Brian. He had been trying to tell me for so long. Over and over. I would not listen. I would not hear him. Another clue I missed. So many times, I missed. His name is not Brian. It was never Brian. It was just a name that sounded like Brian. That was just another misunderstanding, another thing mis-heard by a half-deaf, broken man. My hands shook and twitched. I swallowed the huge knot in my throat. I looked at the battered man crumpled on the dirty floor in this tiny room.

"Orion?" I asked. My voice shook out from my mouth. My soul terrified of the answer.

"Hi Dad." He replied.

16. A MOMENT OF CLARITY

I had always thought I fought for a national pride; stood for an anthem. If I only knew, all along it was a mere ballad of agony.

A symphony of cringe.

I thought I knew pain, physical and mental. I thought I had been toughened. I thought I had descended to the rock bottom depths of suffering. But I had not. It seemed there was a whole new level.

The power of regret was a chasm with no bottom, a freefall in suffering that grew and multiplied in volume and intensity with each plunging inch, with every passing moment. Like a knife, it pierced my heart and called into question everything I had ever done within these walls.

It was all too much. How much suffering could one soul take before it ruptured? How could I have caused such pain, such a level of anguish? How could I hurt and torture someone I did not even know I loved?

I could take no more. Every memory brought only multiplying levels of regret fueled pain. Every nerve was raw. Every thought was torture. So much regret. So much I had done. So much. Too much. Too, too much.

I put the gun in my mouth and clenched my eyes.

"NO!" Orion called out "You can't! Don't!" His voice commanded. "You *OWE* me." Those words froze me. They carried volumes. Those words were deep and paid in a price beyond currency. It was true. I did owe him. "You can't take the easy way out. I won't allow it. After all this, I want my due."

I lowered the gun and looked at the floor.

"I can't...I...what have I done...? I can't even face you. With what I have done to you?" By no means of my own, I crumpled to my knees.

"No. This can't be real. No fucking way." I shook my head back and forth. My mind was fighting for my heart, for a way out of this pain. It's not that I did not believe, I did, I could *feel* it was right. But my mind did not want to. It wanted reprieve from all the terrible things I was guilty of doing to him. All the pain and suffering I had caused. All the hurtful things I said. So, in defense, my twisted mind threw reality into question. "Bullshit!" I half-heatedly argued. "How can this be possible?"

The disbelief overflowed into my rough voice. I was on my feet again. "No. This is just another attempt to get information from me! It *has* to be!"

"I never wanted information. The questions..." He shifted, trying to pull himself more upright. "The questions I asked you were always meant to spark your memories. To get you to remember. To get you to this point, this moment of clarity." He looked at me. His eyes no longer panicked and laced with fear. They were...jubilant.

"You are full of shit!" I put the gun back on him. "You are not Orion! You can't be! Orion is just a child! This is just another mind fuck! An interrogation technique!"

"No. You recalled it properly. The Cuban Operative," he began, "It all started there. 'Operation Cigar,' as you jokingly named it. It never reached phase two. Your team was hit and left for dead." He paused, looking me right in the eye.

"Twenty-eight years ago."

"No." My voice was barely a whisper. My shattered mind reeling and fighting to put it all together.

"It happened just inside the Pakistani border. About twelve kilometers from his suspected position. Only two members of Alpha team survived. Think it through. *Think. Remember…*" he pleaded.

I looked at him. My eyes wide and hungry for the information.

"You, and Postman," he said.

"Postman…" I whispered unintentionally lowering the gun.

"He lost his right arm and suffered burns on sixty-five percent of his body, but he is alive. You though, you were much worse. Not the burns, but the damage. It broke your brain. The burns were on the left side, but that is not where the impact and trauma was."

"Bullshit." I said defiantly.

"Look at your hands. The way they shake and twinge. Can you hear it?" he asked. And I could. Vague and distant. Like before. Just too far away to make out.

"Hold your right hand down by your hip. Then hold your left hand, to the side, away from your chest at shoulder level. Both palms in." He spat blood. "Can you hear it?"

For some reason I followed along, putting my hands in position. I looked stupid, like I was doing an old-time slow dance with an invisible partner. Then my hands twitched, almost in sync. No, wait. It was in sync. Somewhere deep inside I heard that distant melody. Louder and louder, it grew. For the first time I could remember, I could hear it.

"What...in...the..." The gun was still in my right hand, and it felt like it was in the way. I holstered it. As I moved my right hand back into position, I heard the music. I moved my fingers to the G-, then D-, then A-chord.

Then G, D, C.

And repeated G, D, A...

"...*Momma put my guns in the grooound...*" The lyrics left my mouth, barely audible.

"*Cuz, I can't shoot them, anymore...*" Orion filled in the second line. "*Knocking On Heaven's Door.* You loved that song. You were learning to play the guitar. You used it to deal with PTSD and stress when you were on leave. Mom told me you used to lock yourself in the basement and just play that one song for hours. It was working for you. It's why your hands twitch in those strange ways when you are stressed. They twitch to the cords."

I looked down at my hands. Could it be? Or was this just more of his bullshit? Just another scheme? I glanced at my holstered weapon. Was this a way to disarm me? I put my arms down and rose to my feet, pacing back and forth. Visions and memories were flooding back.

"There is no way I have been locked in here for twenty-eight years!" I stared at him. "It has been a year. At the most!"

"President Steve McMillian would not give up on you. He publicly says you ran nine 'world shaping' operations. He hails you as a hero. Publicly. For a politician, that is unheard of. He personally convinced congress and the public to go into Pakistan and get you out. Then, he convinced the Pakistani not just to allow it, but to help. He built this place for you. Unofficially, it's called the

David Richard Ross Mental Facility. Due to the confidential status of your full name, they wanted to name it the Ross Center, but he insisted it be called the D.R. Ross Mental Facility. It was built for you. In his speech he said it was 'To safely hold the most dangerous hero on the planet.'"

"President?" I asked.

"Yes. His actions to free you earned him the respect of the nation and a Presidency."

"Steve?" I asked. "President!?" He nodded. His eyes still watering and his nose slowly dripping blood.

"Alright. Let's say this is not all bullshit. Let's say you are telling me the truth. Why not just come out and tell me all this? Why not just come clean up front and save all this trouble?"

"We tried that." He spat blood on the floor and rubbed his eyes. "It delays the cycles."

"Cycles?"

"Your injury is unique." He wiped the blood from his twisted nose. "I wrote my thesis on it. It goes in cycles. Like a strange form of Alzheimer's. You go into deep delusions for long periods of the time. Then something strikes a memory and you put it all back together." He shifted and swallowed hard. "Like this last one, you are at the end of a cycle where you believed you were a prisoner of war. It's actually your most common one. Every few years you have a moment of clarity and undergo total recall. If we upset it, say by telling you something like 'I am your son' you reject the information as a ploy and it's one less piece of data that can pull you back. So, it takes longer."

"Did you say each cycle is…years?" I gasped. He nodded.

"Your average cycle is about four years. On your second cycle we tried to break you out of it by showing you old pictures and being completely honest with you. It backfired and took you eight years for a moment of clarity."

"How many cycles has it been?"

"Six."

"How long does it last?" I asked. "The moment of clarity?"

"Do you mean, how long do you stay in normal cognition before reverting to the next delusion cycle?" He asked.

"Yes." My voice was dry and quiet.

"A few hours. Usually until you fall asleep."

"You endure *years* of this? Just for a few hours?" I shook my head. A tear crossed my face. "You are a god damned saint. Nothing is worth that."

"Some people are." He smiled. "Not going to lie, this cycle was bad."

"Is this real? I…I can't believe it…" I stammered.

"We tried to help you as much as we could. We gave you all the clues. We put items in place to lead you to this point. The phone was a plant to help jog your memory. Your old truck is in the parking garage, right at the end of the tunnel up on level four. The blueprints were planted to lead you to the truck, not here. I was so sure you would go straight for the garage exit." He shifted again, clearly uncomfortable. "We even left that coating of sand on the floor so you could make the alphabet cyphers."

"I've made those cyphers before?" I asked.

"Yes. You believe the letters you see are a different alphabet, or are encrypted. But they are not. It is just plain English. It is common with a head injury, even with a stroke. You had to learn to read again. For you, it was always just the letters. You are quite resourceful. It is hard *not* to help you, but if we just left you alone with the tools, you always figure it out. You always made a cypher."

"Huh. I hated that layer of sand," I muttered.

"Yeah, it's the desert. There is no escaping it. But at least you are in New Mexico, not the Middle East like you thought." He looked at me through his watering and squinty eyes and he smiled. Not a fake smile, but that contagious kind of uplifting smile. It was infectious. His snowman double dimple beaming at me from the un-bearded side of his face. "This is real. It is the moment I wait all this time for."

"Orion…" I said. "I'm so sorry." I fought back tears. "For everything I have done to you. I thought you were my enemy…"

"Don't be sorry. Every warrior who treads here understands the risks of his journey." I looked at him. I remembered this saying. It was from a familiar place. Was it home? No…

"You used to say that to every new student who started in your martial arts school. I had it made into a scroll. Hung it above the door in the dojo. I have always known what I was getting myself into."

"The dojo is still open? Wait…that's how you learned Bushikan Aikido!" I exclaimed.

"I like to say I have been training in it since before your accident. Remember those videos you used to make to help the remote schools?" Orion asked. I nodded. "I used to watch them all the time. As a kid I loved them. All ninety-six of them, I memorized every one. At about ten years old I started really studying them. Breaking down your movements, angles, and positions trying to figure out how you made it all work and look so easy. It is so fast. When I was about thirteen, I googled your dojo. I was shocked to find one back in Boston. It's not in the same place, but Gus, Rob, and Dutch, your top students, are still teaching and keeping it running. I've trained with them ever since.

"Can I ask you something?" he said as he winced, shifting his injured leg. I nodded. "What triggered your moment of clarity?"

"Dimples." I chuckled pointing to his bare left cheek. He looked shocked for a moment and then grinned.

Next to my foot was the aged, folded paper with the words I FORGIVE YOU scribbled desperately on them. I picked up the paper, unfolded it, and turned it over.

Clashing crayoned lines filled the aged, yellowed page. In the middle, backed by a boxy red, white, and blue flag stood a tan stick figure on a pile of bloody crayon bodies and holding a rifle that was the size of a park bench. At the top of the page, in the blue sky, yellow letters spelled out:

UNVINCIBLE

I could not speak. This was the most valuable thing I had ever held. The weight of the moment robbed me of the ability to do anything but stare at its Crayola beauty.

209

"I'm sorry," Orion said. "We had to lock you up. You gave us no choice. You were violent and determined to get home." Orion shifted again trying to find a position that eased the pain. "But it has not been easy. You can be pretty difficult. And resourceful. Heck, you used a piece of chipped tile to carve those names into your arm."

"Chipped tile?"

"Yeah." Orion chuckled. "We still don't know where you got it. You don't have access to anywhere with tile."

"Heh." I smiled. I had a very strong suspicion where it came from. "Look in front of Jabba's skiff." I chuckled.

"What about the soldiers. The guards. You have to tell them I am sorry. Please…" I pleaded.

"They are volunteers. They know full well who you are and what you can do. Some of them take the job just to meet you; some take it as a challenge. Others for a crack at seeing what the legendary Captain can do. None have left disappointed, and the stories are told for years. Some of them even make the media."

"Screw-arm…that guy was…" I began.

"Deshawn. Yeah, he wanted a crack at you. He is a professional fighter. You know how they are." Orion said. Then he dropped his head. "I'm sorry I tricked you. Sorry I pretended to be Postman. We needed to give you a push." I stared at him for a long moment, then slowly nodded.

"How did you know the countersign?" I asked suddenly thinking of it. Orion looked up.

"From Postman. We had him in the building. He was feeding me lines through an earpiece. So really, you *were* talking to him."

The mention of Postman and the idea of talking to him made me really want to ask about someone else I thought I had been talking to. I held my breath and swallowed deep. I had to know, but was I was also terrified of the answer. Afterall, it had been twenty-eight years.

"Where's Kelly…eh…Mom? Is she ok?" I blurted it out.

He closed his eyes and swallowed hard. "I'm sorry, she's not with us."

"No…" I heard myself say as if I was a thousand miles away.

"Well, she…" Orion began. Suddenly he was cut off by thundering booms on the door behind me. The sound was loud and the concrete floor shook. This was the work of a 'Master Key.' Doors banged open and a team of armed men rushed inside. Chaos reigned, there was shouting to get down, put my hands up, and pleads to wait coming from Orion who was trying to unsuccessfully to stand. Someone asking for Doc's status, more shouts to get down.

I turned slowly and found a familiar face. His eyes traveled from the electrical panel, to me, to Orion where the look on his face morphed into one of sheer terror. I put my hands up in surrender as Gruel's dripping form, donned only with the boxers I left him, raised his gun.

Then fired.

I saw the muzzle flash and felt the punch in the chest. A cry of "NOOOOO!" overtook the ruckus. I stumbled back tripping over a smoldering shovel. As I hit the floor, I caught sight of Orion, running, on his knees at Gruel. It was a knee walking technique called *suwari waza*. Without standing, in a single beautiful motion, Orion disarmed Gruel and threw him, head over heels, with a perfectly executed wrist throw.

"That's my son!" I coughed out. "Look at him god damn it! That's my son!" I barked as something tinny tasting filled my mouth. I spat and noticed the blood. I spat again trying to empty my mouth enough to speak, but it was refilling as fast as I could spit. I drew one last deep breath and coughed out, "That's my hero…look at him…. He's my h…."

Then the world went black.

17. ONE MORE TIME AROUND

Her eyes were wet and she would not look at me. Behind me Orion cried and clung to my leg, his own cries a soundtrack of the emotion in the moment. Outside, the Airport Flight Line van blew the horn again and I held a finger up at the window indicating I needed one more moment.

"You are right." I told her. She finally looked at me.

"I just can't keep doing this," she said. "Look at him. He can't either."

I crouched down and pulled them both in. For a moment, huddled on the floor, we were complete. A family. Something so wonderful it hurt each time someone left even for a moment, let alone months at a time.

"OK," I told them. "Last time. No more." I consoled them both. "We will find another way. Maybe I can work construction with Phil." And for that moment, even facing the uncertainty of a new financial future and life as a civilian, all was right. She smiled that stunning smile and even Orion's wails were lost in the bliss of the moment. Don't get me wrong, it was scary and made me want to puke, but it felt right. And that was wonderful.

"Do you have to go?" she asked.

"I do. But this should be much quicker than last time. We know where this Cuban bastard is this time." I thought about them and I thought about what I was facing. This was going to be easy, quick, and a fitting end to my career. She was right, it was time to stop fighting for others and time to start thinking of myself and my family. It was time for my war to be over. I smiled.

It was going to be alright.

I reached for a deeper hug when something in my chest pulled. The pain twinged deep through my torso, and then flashed down my left side. Instantly my eyes opened and I was hurled from sleep, into the ugly, cruel world.

The low steady tick of a machine mimicked a heartbeat off to my right. Wires and tubes were attached to my right arm and torso. The air was thick with heat and the concrete room was blindingly bright in the mid-morning sun. A low voice came from the foot of my bed. I glanced down to see a man leaning against the bedframe talking on a cell phone. He was mumbling so I turned my head slightly to better hear the conversation.

"Yes. Yes. I know…. He's fine… He is... Yes, he is. Mom, I know… That's OK… I know…I know. Yes, tell Dennis I said hello and thank you. OK, love you. Goodbye." With a finger he punched at the screen of the phone and then slid it into his pocket. Slowly he turned around with the use of a single crutch. The corners of my vision twisted and warped. I drew a deep breath to ask who he was, but as I inhaled, my eyes clenched shut with a brand-new flavor of pain. I reached for the bandages on my chest from where the pain blossomed.

"Whoa, relax. Just take it easy," I think the man said.

"Speak up, stop mumbling!" I barked at him, but my voice came out dry and weak. "Who are you?"

"Ah, sorry." He replied in a louder tone. The man was young, but his eyes were heavy as if he carried a deep burden. He spoke excellent English. He was battered. His nose was taped up, several fingers on one hand were wrapped in a splint, as was his leg. He had numerous stitches and the left side of his clean-shaven face was red and shiny as if it were covered with a lotion for a skin condition. "I am Ryan." I thought I heard him say. Or did he say Brian?

"Where am I?" I hissed out in a whisper. Ryan seemed to sag ever so slightly as his eyes fell to the floor. I tried again to reach for my chest, but once more, was unsuccessful. Something held my arms in place. I looked down to notice the leather shackles wrapped tightly around my wrists.

Ryan hobbled over to the side of my bed. He propped himself up and pulled out a clipboard.

"Tell me Captain, where were you headed in that Humvee?" He asked. Suddenly images flashed in my mind. Fire. Explosion. A phone. A cigar.

WAIT!

We were ambushed.

Oh shit.

I had been captured. I looked around the small concrete room. Power cords ran from outside the small cell, beneath the only door, feeding the machines that I was plugged into. The frame of the bed was chained to the floor and the door looked to be a thick ballistic glass. I thought of my family and my heart sank. I pushed them to the back of my mind. I had to focus.

"Ryan is an American name! Who the hell are you really?" I scolded, but my voice was low and scratchy. "Where is my team? What have you done with them?"

It almost seemed like he started to smile at me, but stopped himself. I glared at him. The thumb of my right hand was sore and stiff. It too, must have been injured in the ambush.

216

"Captain, just relax. I will take care of you. Let's just start with a few questions," Ryan began.

Painfully, I bent the thumb bone unnaturally into the middle of my palm and slowly worked it free of the leather shackle. I smiled at the bastard as my hand subtly came free. I was getting out of here.

I was going to find a way home.

Made in United States
North Haven, CT
09 December 2021

12194156R00124